THE ART OF DEATH

The Nukite kick struck him full-force in the groin. Shreiking in agony, Bartholomew sagged to the deck, a mass of jelly. He twisted and tore at the deck plates with his bleeding fingernails as he died in the lashing rain. But Mace, the Kung Fu Monk-Master, felt no pity.

KUNG FU

#7

C.K. FONG

THE YEAR OF THE COCK

MANOR BOOKS INC.

A MANOR BOOK......1975

Manor Books Inc.
432 Park Avenue South
New York, New York 10016

CHAPTER ONE

There was no moon that night, and by nine o'clock even the stars began to vanish. Cirrus clouds in long gray sheets filled the southwest sky, and then the rain came, not heavy, but cold and penetrating, blowing in from the vast expanse of the Gulf of Mexico to the south.

From where he crouched behind the creosote soaked piling of the jetty, Victor Mace shifted his weight slightly, and continued his surveillance of the dirt roadway that led through the Galveston Island underbrush to the boat shack.

His tension had been mounting for three hours, ever since the blood-red sun had set far off to the west over the flat brutality of the dusty terrain. The man he was waiting to follow was a known murderer. Had he learned that Mace was on his trail? Was that the reason he had not shown up?

The Kung Fu Monk-Master's facial muscles twitched. Instantly he remembered the words of En Sheng, the *Tung-chia* of the Temple:

"The wise man is calm in the face of danger. The fool panics and beckons to death."

A low humming penetrated the rasp of the rain slashing across the surface of the restless Gulf, and Mace moved from the shadow of the piling to watch the probing beams of headlights stab through the slanting rain. He could see the outline of a Buick bouncing over the rutted, uneven road, the springs protesting each time the body slammed down from a rocky obstacle.

He drew back into the shadows as the car pulled up to the boat shack and the doors opened. Two men jumped out. One was a tall, stooped man over six feet in height, and the other was a compact young man with a bull neck and a flat head that seemed to be the working end of a battering ram.

The tall one was Chilson. An underwater demolitions expert from the Vietnam War, he was the man Mace had been detailed to follow tonight. The wiretap tapes had pinpointed Chilson's mission as starting at the jetty here known as Bruce's Fishing Charter.

"It's going to be a pisser of a night," grunted the tall man in a broad Texas accent. "Look at them clouds."

The ram-headed man slammed the door shut and walked around to the trunk. "You're not getting paid to forecast the weather." He spoke in the short clipped tones of an educated man. He pressed back in the darkness.

"Cal," said Chilson softly, "you'd look goddamned funny nine inches shorter. Don't tempt me to pound your head down into your neck."

"Unlace that tarp, will you?" snapped the stocky man. "And shut up. That southwester's enough breeze for me."

Chilson yanked off the end of the tarp.

Mace saw the big man jump down into the runabout, and the short one follow, slinging a canvas bag in behind them. With that, the one Mace thought might be Rice moved to the controls and a moment later the sound of a cold gasoline engine played a counterpoint to the rising wind.

In a minute, the twenty-one foot inboard was throbbing gently, the clouds of exhaust burbling out of the water near Mace's position. Quickly he moved at a crouch away from the pilings to the end of the jetty, where he fastened the nylon line to his waist. The water was cold around the wetsuit, but an extra thickness next to his skin helped insulate him from the chilling effects of the water.

Quickly he attached the nose piece of the re-breather, slipped on the goggles, and ducked below the surface of the water. He could hear the throb of the engine through the rubber hood of the wetsuit, and even the far-off murmur of Lee Chilson's voice.

"Keep the damned engine throttled down. We don't want to alert those Coast Guard bastards."

"Who's in charge of this mission, Lee?"

The water moved about Mace and he could hear the throb of the engine change in timbre. The boat rocked away from the jetty, and the line tautened around Mace's waist. He grasped it with both hands, took double loops around his wrists, and let the surge of the runabout take him in its wake.

He had fastened the tough nylon line to the stern at just about water level where it would not interfere with the propellors of the powerful inboard and where it would be out of sight to occupants of the boat.

The runabout ran slowly out from the shore, bucking the waves that were coming in now with greater and greater frequency and intensity. Mace lifted his head, squinting occasionally through the goggles, to see if the storm was going to make a difference in the night's job. Apparently not.

7

Twenty minutes later he could feel the line loosening as the runabout began circling and the inboard changed its tone. Soon the engine was idling, with the inboard rocking in the increasingly heavy waves being blown across the Gulf by the rapidly approaching storm.

As Mace raised his head from the water he saw a streak of lightning split the sky to the southwest, just over the distant but invisible land mass.

To his left the blue flash painted a scene of unbelievable majesty and power. He knew it was Offshore Drill Platform S 176, but he had never seen it from so close and with such awe inspiring clarity.

It looked like a forest of huge factory chimneys sticking out of the darkened sea, the waves of which were now being smashed against the platform by the wind.

Halfway up the height of these chimneys the gigantic steel platform about a city block in size was held in place.

They neared the rig, the waves slapping at them and driving the nose of the runabout toward the steel legs on the left.

"To starboard," snapped Chilson.

"Stow it," Cal responded.

They passed through the legs and were now under the heavy platform. The waves were pounding with fury against the sea legs, slamming from right to left. Mace raised his head and could see that they were moving slowly toward a portion of the area under the platform where a steel gangway ran down to the level of the sea. It was suspended from a cut out well-deck lower than main platform level.

As the runabout approached the steel gangway, Chilson reached out and grasped the iron rail. Mace could see that Chilson had tied a work belt around his middle, from which hung a half-dozen objects that resembled hand grenades.

The runabout steadied.

"Our guy's name is McCready," the ram-headed man growled.

"I remember."

"He'll lead you to the derrick. You know what to do when you get there."

"You better be waiting. That stuff's set for thirty minutes. I don't want to be trapped here when she blows."

"You're talking to a pro, not some hick greenhorn. Move before I bust you in the chops."

Grudgingly, Chilson clambered over the edge of the runabout and pulled himself up onto the iron steps of the gangway. The ram-headed man busied himself with lashing the runabout to the gangway, pointing the bow into the onrushing waves from the southwest. The wind had begun to howl through the steel legs of the rigging and Mace raised his head once again with satisfaction. The noise afforded by the elements would give him good cover.

His main problem was in keeping out of the sight of the man he thought was Cal Rice while he made his climb after Chilson. Mace watched as Chilson vanished into the darkness above and then he made his move, following along the side of the runabout until he could grip the underedge of the gangway where it reached down into the water.

He watched the boat where the squat man was huddled in the center, his head down to keep it out of the ravaging wind. Then Mace grasped the steel ladder, and began squirming up the underside of it, climbing from one step to the next but keeping himself flat to its silhouette so no movement would attract Rice's attention.

Quickly he scaled the steps, and once in the darkness of the underside of the platform, he climbed

9

over onto the top of the ladder, and advanced the last ten steps at a crouch.

The gangway opened onto a large cutout well-deck. From the well-deck, Mace could see most of the platform. He did not spot Chilson, who was apparently keeping to the shadows himself. Mace assumed a rigid position and did not make a move as he surveyed the scene on the platform.

A hundred yards away, on the main platform to the south stood the derrick itself, looking more massive than ever. Men were moving around near its base. Spaced out at intervals from the base of the derrick were a number of steel cabins, which apparently were storage bins and operating areas.

Under the surface of the platform were living accommodations and the power generating machinery.

Mace turned to the north, and saw that the rest of the platform was almost completely bare. On the well-deck cut into the platform, Mace saw men moving large barrels with the aid of a tracked crane, trundling them into a brightly lit opening halfway along the high bulkhead on the southern part.

They were not oil barrels, Mace knew. These barrels could only contain "mud," a chemical mixture of barites used for forcing down under pressure the cement that formed the outer casing of the drill hole.

Extending along the right of the central well-deck was a series of big storage sheds, most of them open, stretching right across the width of the rig.

Mace could now see a shadowy form loping across the well-deck toward the higher platform where the derrick stood. It was Chilson. Mace moved quickly, running toward the first of the storage bays.

He ducked inside without being seen, and reached in his wetsuit where he brought out a mini-flash wrapped in waterproof plastic. He shone it around the storage bay. It was about a hundred feet long. Stacked in nearly empty racks on both sides were three or four dozens screwed pipes almost as long as the bay itself. Deep gouge marks had been made in each pipe near the end, as if some heavy metal claws had bitten into it.

As Mace turned, he heard a thumping movement near him. Startled, he pulled back into the shadows, trying to make out what had caused the noise. It sounded like the crack of a man's foot against the steel decking.

He waited a few seconds, but heard nothing else. Then he moved around the mountain of pipes and shone the mini-flash into the opaque emptiness.

A man wearing heavy clothing lay trussed up on the steel deck, his mouth taped with wide hospital adhesive.

Mace leaned over him, the mini-flash bright in the florid angry face. It was a typical rigger's face, blue eyed, red nosed, graying at the temples, rugged, wind-burned, sun-tanned. The man to whom it belonged was big muscled and stocky.

Instantly Mace realized that something was wrong. Chilson, running across the well-deck, could not have had time to knock out and bind anyone on the rig. The man had been bound before Chilson came.

Chilson and Rice had spoken of "their man" on the rig. Olsen? If they had a man on the rig, what would be the reason to bind one of the riggers?

Mace shone the light past the big man, and saw another heavy set man trussed up like the first.

The Kung Fu Monk-Master shot to his feet, whirled, and moved quickly to the door of the storage bay. As he broke for the open, a bright light flashed on him from the enormous spotlight mounted to floodlight the entire well-deck.

In the light Chilson stood, grinning at him, not more than ten feet away. The tall man held a Walther PK 9 mm in his right hand, aimed at Mace's neck.

"How does it feel to die, you chink bastard?" Chilson cackled, tensing his finger to pull the trigger.

Mace saw the half dozen men standing in an arc around Chilson, grinning in anticipation of the sight of blood. He had been set up. He, the C.I.A. cell, and the operatives of the Petroleum Institute Security System. The Chilson tapes were phony.

Years of training in the constant anticipation of the unexpected saved Mace's life from the 9 mm slug waiting in Chilson's Walther PK. Before Chilson's finger had squeezed off the shot, Mace was moving, leaping toward him with his left foot traveling in an outside arc, aimed at the wrist of the hand holding the gun.

The *Heti'i* power kick as it struck Chilson's wrist instantly broke both bones and the tall man screamed with agony, gripping his fractured wrist with his left hand. He turned pale and sank back on to the steel decking, writhing in pain.

The Walther, hanging limply from the powerless hand, fired at the instant Mace's kick shattered the wrist, and the slug clanged against the steel bulwark of the platform. It ricocheted into the unfortunate Chilson's right ankle, breaking the ankle bone and smashing the flesh.

A burly tough pounced on the Walther PK, moving as quickly as he could to secure the weapon and waste Mace before he could protect himself.

Mace's trained brain was far ahead of the burly goon, whom Mace now guessed had been hired, along with the rest of those facing him, to help spring the trap into which he had been so skillfully

lured. As the muscled man scooped up the Walther
PK, crouching on the deck on hands and knees, lifting the barrel at Mace, the Kung Fu Monk-Master
dived forward, his right hand cocked in a *Nukite*
blow which caught the would-be gunman frontally
in the throat, crushing his Adam's apple. The
Walther PK 9 mm slipped to the platform and the
dying man grabbed at his neck as the blood poured
up into his throat, choking him to death on his own
vital fluids.

By now the circle of hired thugs had broken apart.
These trained killers were professionals. They did
not run away. They were immediately aware of the
danger at the hands of the foe who had already
stopped two men armed only with his hands.

An ex-hood named Pinky Desnoyers was the next
who reacted with dispatch. An albino, he dyed his
hair red to make himself presentable to his fellow
man. Desnoyers went nowhere without a snubnosed
S and W .45 caliber revolver clipped to his shoulder
holster.

When he saw Chilson go to the steel deck with his
gun hand dangling, Desnoyers instantly flipped open
his sports jacket and grabbed the Smith and Wesson
.45. In the split second it took Mace to finish off
Chilson with his leaping foot blow, Desnoyers had
got the handgun into position to fire. He fired.

Mace was not there. Seeing Desnoyers out of the
corner of his eye, the Kung Fu Monk-Master spun
on his heel and jumped high in the air, administer-
ing a *Wa Lu-Ti* Dragon Foot snap kick, instantly
paralyzing the solar plexus, rupturing the abdominal
wall, and hemorrhaging the gunman's vital organs
internally.

Desnoyers crumpled to the deck, the S and W firing into the air. He lay there in the pelting rain as
the life slowly ebbed out of him, the flow of blood

pumping out onto the steel deck, flooding the S and W on which he lay.

Nick Bartolomew was next to join the surging attack on the Kung Fu Monk-Master. Armed with a twelve inch flyssa, a Moroccan sword characterized by a single-edged blade engraved and inlaid with brass, Bartolomew slid it histily from the scabbard he wore around his waist and came at Mace with a wild glare.

"Your last breath on earth, you chink son of a bitch!" he yelled, and slid the deadly blade upward toward Mace's groin. But the Kung Fu *Tung-chia* had anticipated the black-haired ex-con's move with the blade, and countered by whirling around with a simple *Korsi Tu Minga* kick to the crotch.

Shrieking in agony, Bartolomew sagged to the deck, his sexual apparatus a mass of jelly instantly radiating pain from its ruined center to every nerve ending in his body. As he fell, the ugly flyssa impaled him in the heart as he sank down face first. He twisted and tore at the deck plates with his bleeding fingernails as he slowly lost consciousness and died in the lashing rain.

By now the remaining professionals had withdrawn to the shadows to organize a counterattack on the "crazy goddamned gook," as one of them characterized Victor Mace.

Abu Sikkam, a Moslem born in the slums of Constantinople and imprisoned for life for murder in his youth only to escape in a political uprising in Turkey and make his way through the underground to America, was the canniest of the remaining thugs. He was also in charge of the fifteen-man group that had taken over the rig.

He waved them into the shadows of the well-deck and vanished after them.

Mace realized that the remaining numbers of the

enemy corpus were regrouping for attack.

"In war," En Sheng had once said, "there is no respite. The warrior who rests to recoup his strength is inviting the devil to take him. The time to rest is after the war is won. The war against evil is never won. Remember that, my son."

It would be best to escape now from the platform, grab the runabout, and get back to shore. Although Mace was dressed in his wetsuit, and could swim great distances because of his years of training, he did not intend to swim back to the shore in the fury of the storm.

He must overpower Rice who was obviously guarding the runabout and make his way back by boat. He must bring news of the attempted ambush to his C.I.A. contacts and the P.I. Security leader. If this attack was a feint, the real attack on the petroleum industry would be somewhere else.

Mace skidded across the bloodied deck and grabbed the iron handrail of the gangway leading down into the water. Across the expanse of the deck the wind and rain slashed at him, blowing the torn garments of the four dead men and soaking them in chilling rainwater.

He gained the gangway and was ten steps down when he saw the form of Rice coming up toward him from below.

"You chink jerk," Rice yelled, "how'd you get away?" He was holding a deadly Czechoslovakian 9 mm Schlaglemilch in his hand, lifting it to aim at Mace's midsection.

Hanging onto the metal rail with one hand, Mace jumped from the step he had reached and let his left foot take Rice in the temple with a *Chungdan Ap Chago*, a middle-front snap kick. At the same instant, Mace arched around to the side and flung himself out of the path of the ascending man's line of sight.

That was when the slug from the Czech murder weapon spiraled up into the heavens, sizzling harmlessly through the lashing rain. Rice's skull snapped like a cracked egg. The cry that rose to his throat died as he slipped away from the steps and sagged onto the gangway draped over a steel step. The automatic fell into the spuming water below.

Mace pushed past, hurrying down the steep incline to the runabout which he could see bobbing in the darkness below.

Then suddenly he was hanging in the air, a thick rope looped around his neck and pulling as tight as a hangman's noose. Mace swung like a pendulum, halfway the victim of a lynch mob, halfway a corpse already.

It was Buck Catlin who had roped Mace the same way he had roped many a steer in his time. Catlin was a rodeo star who had hit the skids due to a combination of alcoholic indulgence and a predilection for extremely tough pussy. Drifting into the nether world of Dallas, he had eventually joined up with a group of barroom hoodlums who made their living scrounging for the buck here and there as hit men, heisters, and scam artists of all kinds.

"Pull it tight!" Sikkam shouted, as Mace swung there in the darkness, hardly knowing what had happened to him. Catlin yanked and several other hands joined in to pull Mace into the air where he dangled helplessly.

"That's one less goddamned chink in the world," shouted Goose Bandy, a moronic pimp who had spent three quarters of his life in prison, but was fatefully out in the street now.

"Haul him up!" shouted Sikkam triumphantly.

The goons gathered around him, grinning as the rain lashed down at them, the wind blowing their clothes and hair wildly. Lightning forked down from the sky, splitting the night and illuminating the towering derrick above them.

They pulled hard, jerking and twisting at the rope.

"Make sure he's dead!" yelled Sam Riley, known as One-Ball Riley ever since he had been partially maimed by the disgruntled husband of a floozie he had been caught in bed with one eventful evening.

"He's dead," chortled Buck Catlin, as the figure of the slender half-Chinese, half-American was dragged up over the edge of the gangway and onto the steel deck where the rain slammed down at the closed Oriental eyes and expressionless face.

One-Ball Riley ran across the platform and yanked the fatal flyssa out of Bartolomew's dead body, and ran gleefully toward the prone Monk-Master.

"No!" Sikkam shouted, grabbing One-Ball by the arm. He knew the womanizer's predilection for emasculating anyone he took a disfavor to. "He's going into the water whole! We don't want anything left of him to show he's been here, do we?" He grinned at the crowd of toughs.

"Right!" bawled Catlin.

"Take the noose off his throat," snapped Sikkam. "You, Cat."

Catlin leaned down over the body on the deck, and gripped the noose, pulling it back from the bulging throat muscles. It was his last move in life. Instantly a forefinger and middle finger of the far from dead Victor Mace formed a deadly *Nihon*—and caught the bulldogger's Adam's apple, forcing the muscles into paralysis. Then, with deadly *Chungdan Sudo Yop Taerigi*, a middle knife-hand strike, Mace speared the throat above the Adam's apple, killing the bulldogger instantly.

17

The moment the noose had tightened around Mace's throat, he had instantly employed the psychic force of *chi* to expand the throat muscles enough to keep the noose from cutting off his wind and crushing his Adam's apple.

He forced the *chi* deep into all parts of his body from the inner centers of the thalamus, feeling the impulses of strength radiating outward through his body, moving into the chest and the throat. And with the *chi* came the intensification of the *teh*, the determination for truth and right possessed by all men but which only the trained few are able to use effectively.

The noose loosened as the throat muscles swelled to protect the vital arterial and nervous system running through the throat. Mace closed his eyes, "playing possum," as his American compadres said. The men on the rig would consider him dead when they hauled him up to the deck.

In a moment he felt himself being raised upward, exactly as he had anticipated. Then he was laid out on the deck.

Still he did not move. The rope snugged his throat. He did not want to risk shrugging out of it at the same time he must handle half-a-dozen attackers.

Then he leaped up, using a blindingly quick succession of *Nukite* blows to one man's heart, killing him, and an *Empi* elbow smash to another man's abdominal wall, paralyzing the victim's solar plexus and leaving him half sunk to the steel deck with his eyes wide open and his face frozen in shock for eternity.

Mace grabbed another man, using *Hsing-I*, a form of boxing in which one punches against the internal organs and not against the external framework. He screwed his fist as he stabbed out at his antagonist's

18

midriff, the sudden twist rupturing the man's liver and leaving him to sink through the air, the pain of his agonized vitals pinwheeling out to every portion of his body as he collapsed in death.

Heti'i power kicks to a head and to a neck sent two men sliding across the steel deck, senseless. One skidded over the edge and plunged down into the water below without even knowing he was going to drown. The other fell to the steel gangway and broke his back on one of the steps, then hung there.

Mace was on his feet when One-Ball Riley threw the wicked flyssa blade through the air at him. Only by leaping to one side was Mace able to avoid being speared through the heart with the steel blade.

As it was, the blade tore at the wetsuit and was deflected from his body at the moment a heavy black suddenly charged head-first into Mace, using football field tactics in the hope of knocking the slender Oriental down.

The flyssa sliced through his jugular with a clean, slippery sound, and fell to the deck. So did the black's head, which had been neatly severed from his body.

Mace stared a moment at the headless body spurting blood from the pulsating corpse.

Mace could not make out his enemies. It seemed everyone on the platform was no longer moving. He remembered Riley, who had thrown the knife at him, although he did not know him by name. He remembered one other in particular, the large Islamic type who had taken command of the stragglers. And he remembered one other—a freckle-faced Irishman who had stood back and watched the events with amusement bordering on the insane.

Clarence Finn, known as Huck Finn throughout his rambunctious, hell-raising life, had an ace up his sleeve. It was he who had rescued the Walther PK from the steel deck of S 176. It had amused him to watch the yellow menace deal death to so many of the slobs who had been with him through the night waiting to massacre the halfbreed kid from Hong Kong.

Finn was no fool. He knew the slant-eyed piss-cutter would ruin anyone who went up against him in fair combat. The thing to do was to gun him down from ambush. The problem was that the gook would instantly spot him if he tried to shoot in plain view. He had to stash himself somewhere and wait.

When the Kung Fu Monk-Master came to life after being lynched in the rainstorm, Finn knew that his way was now clear. He jumped down the gangway, descended the steps, and jumped into the runabout he found lashed to the steel railing.

Under a piece of tarp he hid himself, with the Walther PK in his hand, lying there and waiting for the form of the halfbreed to climb down into his hail of 9 mm bullets.

Chilson had crawled painfully across the well-deck, to find his way onto the large platform that supported the oil derrick. He lay in the shelter of one of the control cabins near its base. The pain from his shattered wrist and bloody ankle was nauseating him. He vomited and then fell into his vomit. It was there that serried waves of ultimate pain engulfed him, sending him into brief shock and then into unconsciousness.

He did not even feel it when he slid down onto the rainpelted deck and cracked his skull on the steel plates.

Abu Sikkam huddled in the darkness of the storage bay housing the drill pipes. With him were One-Ball Riley and Goose Bandy. The big Moslem was sick with annoyance.

"Where the hell did that damned Walther 9 mm

go to?" he growled, tweaking his spade beard with a flicking forefinger. "I never brought a piece because that damned slob Chilson said we wouldn't *need* guns! He said he'd kill the chink bastard if we couldn't tear him to pieces ourselves!"

Goose Bandy was shivering. "Shee—it! The damned Walther must of slid into the Gulf, man. T'ain't our fault we got no weapons. That noodle-lover just been lucky so far!"

"Sure," snapped One-Ball Riley. "*You* go out and take care of him!"

There was a short silence.

Sikkam got up and moved toward the opening of the storage bay. "Where in hell is he?" He peered out. The wind howled, the rain slammed down, the lightning flashed. There was no one out there still able to move about, except the Moslem and the fat man. He knew exactly where they were. They were in the storage shed next to him. He had pressed his ear against the wall and heard them talking. Mace knew why Sikkam had sent Bandy out to reconnoiter. He knew what would happen to Bandy, knew it as well as he knew his own name.

The wind tore at his clothes as Goose Bandy slipped and slid down the one hundred and thirty-nine steps to the runabout. The waves were slamming into the steel supports of the rig with increasing intensity as he came closer to the water's level, where foam and spume were being hurled into the air by the freak turns and twists of the wind.

The Chinaman? Where was he?

"Come out, you chinko!" he screamed, the wind hurling his words away. "Come out and get what's good for you!" He drew out the heavy wrench he had picked up in the storage shed and waved it over his head.

The tarpaulin in the runabout moved.

Bandy smashed down with all his might on the form inside the tarp just as the Walther spewed forth its last three 9 mm slugs directly in Bandy's face. The slugs tore through his face between his eyes, popped his skull and removed the top half of his head which vanished in a spray as fine and as the spume of the Gulf of Mexico in which it was carried off.

The wrench slid from his hands and fell on top of the corpse of Huck Finn, whose neck had been broken instantly when the head of the wrench slapped into his fifth vertebra. His corpse wore the enigmatic Irish grin with which he had observed the mundane earth for the forty-five years of his alcoholic, brawling, ineffectual life.

Abu Sikkam heard the three shots and turned to One-Ball Riley. "You hear that?"

"I heard it!" sniggered Riley.

Sikkam grabbed Riley and danced around with him. "We got the son of a bitch!"

"Come on! Let's get out of here and grab the runabout. I've had it!"

They ducked their heads as they emerged onto the rainswept deck. Neither saw the form in front of them.

One flying wheel throw hold, with Mace's left leg next to One-Ball Riley's right leg, and Riley went flying sideways, sliding across the deck and dropping over the edge, screaming, into the fury of the storm-beaten ocean.

And a split second later, a middle spear-finger thrust to the right side of Abu Sikkam's throat and the big Moslem sank down on his knees, facing Mecca, his right carotid artery punctured and presaging instant death.

If Mace's count was right, that took care of everyone except the two trussed-up guards. It would be better if they did not know who had walked away from the rig under his own power.

Mace sauntered to the gangway, glancing about at the carnage, and slowly descended the steel steps to the runabout. Clearing it of its offensive burden, he settled down at the controls and flicked the line from the steel rail. A moment later the engine started. He headed the craft into the rolling waves and circled around toward Galveston Bay.

CHAPTER TWO

Tom Galey lit a cigarette nonchalantly, gazing about him at the good looking girls—there were always good looking girls at Intercontinental in Houston—and admiring openly their legs and breasts. He was, as always, playing the role of the healthy, hearty all-American boy.

Several people moved toward Gate 18. Without seemig to, Galey cast a quick expert glance over every one of them. Father and son, waiting obviously for the return of some family member from overseas. Woman of middle age with mother of old age, probably meeting a husband returning from a business trip. Two Chinese men dressed in sharp New York/ London clothes, obviously in the oil business and about to meet a co-worker from the People's Paradise. And several stragglers who might have been down to see the sights.

Galey knew the two Chinese. They worked for Sumatro, a small Chinese-owned and English-operated oil firm with a branch office in Houston. They were clean. The People's Republic had cleared them in the dossiers on microfilm in Galey's confidential files. The firm produced only about 250,000 barrels a day, but was important for its tie-in with the British Government.

The first of the arrivals strolled out of the red carpeted accordion chute, glancing about them self-consciously as they sought friends or the sign pointing to the baggage check-in. The ninth man out was the Major.

Galey recognized him instantly. He had studied the photographs carefully, and there was no mistaking the barrel chested frame, the big-boned bulk, the neckless body, the heavy head with jug ears sticking out from the slick black hair combed down over the forehead like a Chinese version of Adolf Hitler.

At six feet four, Major Hsung Fong resembled the monster in Frankenstein, with the same lumbering gait, the same determined, deadly serious manner, the same frozen fish-eyed face, the only exception being the slant of the Major's Chinese eyes—and perhaps the lack of the bolt through the monster's neck.

A god-damned Chinese hill bandit, thought Galey languidly. And to a certain extent he was right. Major Fong had made the Long March with Chiang Kai-shek before the general had broken with the Kuomintang and established the Chinese Nationalist Party, which now existed in exile on Taiwan, or Formosa, with 16,000,000 Chinese Nationalists under him.

The impassive slitted eyes roved quickly about the interior of the International Arrivals Building, passed over Galey's face, and went on for a full second before returning and riveting to it. Major Fong approached Galey slowly, face absolutely expressionless.

"Good evening," he said in very bad English. "It is a pleasure to greet you, Captain Galey."

Galey glanced frantically about, seeing with relief that they were quite isolated.

"It is a pleasure, Major," Galey said rapidly in excellent Chinese, his voice low. "It would please me greatly if you did not refer to my rank *even in Chinese*. I am sure you understand the problem." Then, switching to English, he said slowly, "Come with me, Mister Fong. As soon as we collect your baggage, we'll drive into town. I have my car."

Major Fong seemed amused. He nodded and fell into step with Galey, who began walking toward the baggage room.

"My dear Mister Galey," he said in Chinese. "Those who do not know who you are do not care.

A dangerous man, Galey decided. Not a flicker of warmth in the eyes. Not a sign of a smile on the mouth. Not an ounce of humanity evident. Galey shivered.

As they waited for the baggage to appear and slide down the trough into the large plastic lazy susan that rotated around the spout, the Major spoke softly in Galey's ear.

"We were shocked at the death of Major Quon and the penetration of the cell," he said quickly. "I mean to—"

"If you please," Galey responded, "we will talk about this later?"

The Major's eyes narrowed to slits. His expression froze at the implied reprimand from an obvious inferior—not only an inferior, but a member of the hated Caucasian race, at that.

"Who can hear?" The Major glanced about in contempt. "Only stupid Americans!"

"Stupid perhaps, Major," Galey said flatly, his voice sing-song and in complete control, yet underlaid with iron. "But while we are in my court, we play the game my way."

27

There was a pause during which Galey could feel shivers running up and down his spine. Finally the Major got himself in control.

"Very well then, if you insist on playing the role of a bourgeois capitalist pig."

Galey grinned. "That's more like it, Major."

They stared at one another for a long moment, in which Galey could feel heat rise in his cheeks and then suddenly recede.

In silence they waited for the bags to bound down and drop into the circling carrier. Galey grabbed the two with the Major's tag and carried them toward the exit to the parking lot.

"You put me in a Cadillac and you want me to act like a peasant!" Fong said, when Galey motioned him into the front seat.

"In a land of mudhens, the peacock is out of place," said Galey.

Shaking his head, Major Fong climbed out, braced himself against the wind, and climbed in front next to Galey. Galey started up the car, let it purr a moment in neutral, and then moved the automatic control to D. The Cadillac glided smoothly ahead through the rain.

Once on U.S. Highway 59 on the way to Houston, Major Fong gazed at Galey and studied him a long, penetrating moment. Galey pretended not to notice.

"The General was most upset to learn that the Kung Fu Monk-Master had been sent to Houston. He has been known to work hand in glove with the C.I.A. pigs. Would you please outline your plans to destroy this Nationalist devil?"

Galey repressed a smile. He kept his eyes on the road ahead, where the storm was raising hell with the pavement and with his windshield wipers.

"The matter of the Kung Fu Monk-Master has been taken care of, Major Fong," he said softly. "In fact, by the time we arrive at the spread, I hope to have word of the success of the mission."

A faint smile appeared on the Major's rock-hard face. "And what type of elimination had you planned, Captain?"

"The Houston C.I.A. long ago penetrated our established cell, Major. The infiltrator planted a wire-tap before he was isolated and whiffed." Galey frowned. "We allowed the tap to remain."

Major Fong grimaced in what Galey felt might be a smile of amusement. "You force-feed specific information through that channel. Am I right, Captain?"

Galey nodded. "So we let Benny Juarez tape us discussing an operation involving S 176."

"Who is 'Juarez' and what is 'S 176'?"

Galey explained that Benito Juarez was the C.I.A. chief of station in Houston, responsible directly to the D.O.D. Hub, and that the S 176 was an offshore oil rig not far from Galveston Island in the Gulf of Mexico.

"The so-called idea was to sabotage the rig, blow it up," Galey chuckled. "I've got two men, one an experienced underwater demolitions man who had been cashiered out of the Navy, and a torpedo from Chicago. We pretended they were going out to blow up the platform."

"But for what purpose?"

Galey laughed. "Does it matter? We tied it in with Major Quon's death, and they fell for it."

"You were sure of this Kung Fu Monk-Master?"

"We knew sabotage was right up his alley. Sure enough, Juarez immediately put Mace on the job."

"And he swallowed the bait?"

"Like a good little fish. My contact phoned me at nine-thirty and said the two were headed out to the rig in the runabout, with the half-breed towing himself by a nylon line. I expect the work took scant time. The operation on board the rig had gone as expected. At nine-fifteen I was told that they had taken over from the night guards as planned."

"If Mace has been eliminated, that makes our work that much easier." Major Fong was breathing a bit more freely now. "I don't mind telling you, we all lost a night's sleep when you messaged us that Mace was on the scene." Major Fong turned sharply toward Galey. "How in the world did Major Quon ever allow himself to be taken?"

Galey sucked in his breath. "It was a freak accident, sir. One of the cannisters failed to ignite in a test Major Quon was supervising. When his demo man refused to inspect it, the Major was forced to go himself. The damned cannister blew with Quon within the area of total penetration. He was killed, but not destroyed. The police came up with an identification. Juarez got into the case when the Houston Police Department discovered the victim was Chinese. And then Juarez put together a composite on Quon and called the Hub. They sent out Mace to trace back along the line to find out what Quon was doing in Houston."

"Has Operation Lamp been compromised?" Major Fong asked with a steely glint in his eye.

"No sir." Galey looked him in the face.

Major Fong glared at Galey for a moment.

"We shall soon find out if you are telling the truth," he commented. "That's the reason the General sent me to *advise* you for the duration of the operation." The word "advise" was definitely underlined.

"Yes sir." Galey looked bleak.

"We will discuss it later." The Major waved his hand.

Galey turned the Caddy onto Mt. Houston Road.

"This is the way to the spread."

"What is a 'spread'?" Major Fong inquired after a moment.

"It's a ranch," said Galey. "I purchased it from a cattle man who moved to Vermont after making his pile. It's remote enough, right on Lake Houston, but not too far from town. And it's quite well protected, as you can see once you're there. Electrified fence, Doberman pinschers patroling at all hours, heat detectors in every square inch of the walls, constant video surveillance, with a man on the tube at all hours, triple locks on every door and window, and all the latest in burglar alarms."

"One tends to distrust too much technology," muttered Major Fong.

"Wait till you see it! It's a fortress!"

"I hope so, Captain Galey." Major Fong leaned back and closed his eyes. "Colonel Dungjing requested me to convey his best wishes and felicitations."

Galey relaxed. Colonel Dungjing was an old friend, the man who had recruited Galey into the select ranks of the Social Affairs Department.

"I return the compliment."

Major Fong ticked the points off in a musical singsong. "Shot down over Vietnam six years ago, sent to Hanoi and given psychological profile tests, transferred to espionage school in Peking with two other captured Americans, schooled and trained for three years, and then returned to the United States with the celebrated prisoner exchange in 1973." Major Fong opened his eyes lazily. "Correct, Captain?"

Galey nodded. They had a dossier on him in Peking, of course. General Hap-sung, the Director of Intelligence Operations, had the facts correct.

"Here we are," Galey said as he turned the Cadillac into the entrance to the spread after crossing the

San Jacinto River. Yellow headlights cut through the slashing rain, revealing a hurricane fence twelve feet high, split where the road went through by a high gate that had a sign in the middle:

LAZY G RANCH
ABSOLUTELY NO ADMITTANCE!

Galey reached for the dashboard and pressed a button that had been mounted near the hood release. The gate ahead of them suddenly stirred and swung to the left, leaving the roadway open.

Major Fong grunted with interest. "Ahah! The miracles of decadence!"

The Cadillac shot through the opening and Galey pressed the button twice. Behind him, in the rearview mirror, he watched the gate swing shut and lock. He drove ahead, winding through low shrubbery in a garden up to a large rambling structure with stucco walls and Spanish tiles on the roofs of the Lazy G Rancho.

Galey parked in the garage and let the Major out of the car. Together they walked through a door at the side of the garage that led into the rear of the house. A man in a turtleneck shirt and dungarees appeared. He had close-cropped hair of a pepper and salt nature and a face that had been the veteran of scores of ring encounters, some of them very rough. What was left of his face resembled sandpaper. His eyes were green.

"Get the bags out of the car, Bish."

Bish nodded, caught the keys Galey threw at him, and disappeared.

"Is he secure?" Major Fong asked.

"As safe as houses," responded Galey. "The day Bish goes, we'll all go."

Major Fong nodded.

A Mexican girl about eighteen with black eyes and hair combed and knotted it in the back, came up to

32

them as they entered the living room. "Phone call, Mr. Galey."

Galey nodded, his eyes brightening. "It's probably Chilson."

It was not Chilson. It was the Texas Medical Center. They had a man named Lee Chilson under heavy sedation. He had been found on the platform of an off shore drilling rig. There had been an unexplained tragedy during the storm. Everyone on the rig was dead except for two guards who had been rescued by the Coast Guard cutter. Chilson was suffering from concussion, broken wrist, fractured tibia and crushed right tarsus.

According to the guards only one man had gotten away alive. He was someone who might be half Chinese . . .

"Mace!" whispered Galey.

"What about him?" snapped Major Fong.

"The son of a bitch is alive!"

Major Fong's eyes flashed and he swelled up like a toad. "You imbecile! I'm taking over. From now on you take orders from me. No compromise!"

"The hell you are!" yelled Galey.

"I'll send a message to the General!" raged Major Fong. "*Then* you'll see!"

"Until then I'm still in charge!"

"What about your crew of killers?" Major Fong asked, making a chopping motion with his hands as if he were axing a board in a karate hack. It was a gesture that seemed to be a habitual one with him.

Galey could hardly speak. "They're all dead—except for one man!"

Galey sank into the couch as Major Fong shrugged out of his proletarian overcoat and removed his *caracul* hat carefully. He stood in the middle of the room in his dull People's Paradise clothes and glowered at Galey.

"I'm sending a cipher to General Hap-sung to-night! This operation is one of the most important in the history of the People's Republic! I never did understand how an American like you was put in charge of it. As for Major Quon, the man was a fool. No one but a fool could have got himself blown up by a bomb of his own construction! Millions of dollars of investment depend on the success of this project. Do you understand me, Captain Galey?" Galey opened his mouth to speak, but no words came.

"What are you going to do about it?" Major Fong cried, coming over and grabbing the lapels of Galey's sharp new jacket. Galey stared, his eyes popping. "I—I—"

Major Fong jounced him up and down until Galey's teeth rattled.

"Well?"

Galey gripped Major Fong's wrists with an intensity of desperation and removed his hands from his lapels.

"What are you going to do about this Kung Fu Monk-Master?"

"Destroy him," said Galey, thinking fast, but grasping nothing but air in his desperation.

"How?"

"With the principles of seek and destroy," Galey responded, popping up with an old phrase from his Vietnam days.

"Birdshit!" snarled Major Fong. "I asked you *how*!"

"I—I—In the usual way one destroys a cock of the walk."

"Cock of the walk?" Major Fong repeated, puzzled.

"Yes!" cried Galey in a flash of inspiration. Major Fong's epithet had activated his imagination. Bird. Fowl. Rooster. Cock.

34

"And how is that?" Major Fong began to sound like Socrates, Galey thought. He did not say so.

"What causes the cock to crow?" Galey asked.

Major Fong's jaw dropped open. "What are you braying so emptily about?"

"In the dialogue of the Chairman," Galey said rapidly. " 'What causes the cock to crow?' 'The rise of the morning sun.' 'And what causes the morning sun to rise?' 'The turn of the world.' 'And what causes the world to turn?' 'Love.' 'And what has love to do with the crowing cock?' 'Ask the chicken.' "

Major Fong's face turned slowly red and his breathing increased until it seemed he would explode.

Galey held up his hand.

"I have such a chicken, Major."

"You had better have."

"And with the chicken we'll catch the cock so he crows no more."

CHAPTER THREE

Benito Juarez was chief of Houston's Central Intelligence Agency base. The base was of course well camouflaged, as all local cells of the C.I.A. are. The Houston station was opened on order of the Domestic Operations Division after a group of abortive assassination attempts on Fidel Castro in Cuba, would-be killings that were mistakenly attributed to C.I.A. agents.

The resulting furor in Cuba and the dissemination of counter-agents and fellow travelers—one of whom was said to be Lee Harvey Oswald—prompted the Director to open a window on the western Caribbean in Houston, where its port at Galveston and its N.A.S.A. services could afford excellent observation facilities.

Benito Juarez was chosen from a list of possible chiefs of station and sent down to open and operate the base for as long as it proved necessary. Located in a ground-floor store front on Congress Street, in the older part of Houston, the World Travel Service was just slightly dingy, just slightly cheap, and just slightly inept so that most travelers with any sense left it strictly alone and chose the more affluent and enterprising ones up and down the lanes nearby.

In the back section of Benny's World Travel Service was the safe house—a group of rooms that formed a spacious apartment with stairs up into a back loft entered only by the front rooms. It was here, in a cell with no windows and no access other than a front door that the pod met when it had to.

"Why the hell you call the Agency a pod?" asked one exasperated visitor from the Hub.

"Houston fuzz once called us 'as dumb as peas in a pod,' " Juarez responded with some malice. "I liked that. So from then on we've been the pod."

The Hub visitor shook his head in disgust. "The Director wouldn't like it."

"When he finds out I'll know who told him," Juarez observed with those Aztec eyes glittering behind the mineral facade of his countenance.

"One-thirty," Benny Juarez said now, glancing once again at his wrist watch. "Should be getting here."

In the pod now—the no-access room was also called the pod—were four men. Opposite Juarez at the long table sat Daniel S. Bolton, a barrel-chested dude with stork legs and a long flat head that looked like an axe blade. Bolton's nose was as long and sharp as Juarez's was flat and wide. An incompetent dentist had allowed his two top incisors to protrude like Bugs Bunny's. In spite of his mole-like appearance, he was anything but fearful and spookish.

He talked in a harsh Texas accent replete with crude epithets and ejaculations. His manners were those of the stable, where he had been brought up on his uncle's ranch in the Staked Plains. Bolton had served in the Marines, with valor, for he was a man who liked nothing better than a fight to the death. He thrived on blood. He salivated to punch and maim and hurt.

As a Texan and all-American hero of authentic record, he hated thieves, prostitutes, rich men, foreigners, spiks, greasers, and gooks with equal intensity. As chief of the S.S.—Security System—of the Petroleum Institute, he rode herd over fifty operatives throughout the United States, whose job it was to protect the security of the many branches of oil companies which were members of the P.I.

"Stinking chinko should of phoned in when he hit the beach again," growled Bolton, picking his teeth with a gold toothpick he had been awarded by the Houston Police Department for the murder of a would-be oil truck hijacker in a fiery ambush.

"And compromise the pod?" Juarez wondered, not bothering to look at Bolton.

Bolton hissed an expletive in his teeth and continued with the gold pick, probing now at his tooth.

The third man in the room was a red-headed giant with the map of Ireland rolled out over his puss. Maury Quinn was as volatile as Juarez was impassive. An ex-alcoholic, he had almost been given up for lost when he had dried out for the last time in an Austin sanitarium. After that Juarez, who had worked with him in Dallas as an oil roustabout, had put him to work in the pod.

Quinn's concentration on the work took his mind off alcohol, and he had rehabilitated himself. Quinn was an instinctive fighter. He had the fastest reflexes Juarez had ever seen—except for Mace's, of course. He had also the sharpest eyes, and the quickest ears. In fact, Quinn was a machine of muscle and nerve, the sinews of which had been tested and proved many times over.

"He's coming," growled Quinn.

Bolton turned with a stare. "What're you, Mickey Finn? Some kind of god damned seer?"

39

"I hear the minibus," Quinn replied softly.

The fourth man, Hank Shatford, Bolton's right hand man, sat up straight. He was wiry and tall, with a long face and a bald head. In his twenties, he looked forty. Liquor, women, and too much good living had simply short-circuited his aging processes so that he resembled a man going down the other side of life.

"You can't hear through walls!" he snorted at the big Irishman.

Quinn said nothing.

"What do you want to bet the chink blew the gig," said Bolton, examining with interest the gold toothpick, and removing a piece of half-rotted celery from it.

"What is it you have against Victor Mace?" Juarez asked affably, his eyes burning against the light into Bolton's.

Bolton straightened in the chair, realizing that Benny Juarez in his quiet way was challenging him.

"The jerk's a chink, ain't he? What kind of deal is it sending some gook out on a job we could have done!"

"We?" Quinn softly countered. "It's out of your jurisdiction, Danny."

"It's attempted sabotage of an oil rig!" shouted Bolton. "I'm in charge of security—"

"Not on this one," Juarez said firmly. "The pod intercepted that message from the tap on a Sinotex K.A."

"Known Agent!" snarled Bolton. "How do you know that chink at Sinotex is a known agent? He might be setting you up!"

Juarez leaned back. "Of course it might be a set-up, Danny. But that's what we've got to find out, isn't it?"

"If they did manage to sabotage that rig—" Bolton began. A red light over the one door blazed on.

"It's Mace," said Juarez, rising.

Every eye in the room turned to the door. Juarez moved across the room and lifted the small cover of the eye-hole in the center of the cold-rolled steel encased door.

He could see the Chinese Monk-Master standing in the identification zone before the door, which was hidden at the back of a storage closet at the rear of the World Travel Service office.

Juarez pressed the button hidden under the surface of the door frame to the right of the latch and the door slowly swung outward. Mace moved around it lithely and smiled at Juarez with only faint expression.

The door closed behind him.

"Well?" said Juarez, unable to withhold interest.

Slowly the Kung Fu Monk-Master moved to the empty chair beside Juarez's desk where he sat and faced the rest of them. For a moment he let his eyes travel over the faces of those watching him and then he turned to the Mexican-American.

"It was a set-up."

"Shee-it!" cried Shatford.

"I told you so!" boomed Bolton, coming up out of his chair and waving his right hand over his head in a fist. "You damned dumb C.I.A. knee-jerk liberals —"

"Juarez raised a hand for silence.

Almost strangling, Bolton went back into his seat. He leaned forward, his sharp face flushed, his eyes almost red with excitement.

"The man named Rice is dead."

Someone let out his breath audibly.

"Chilson may be dead. I tried not to kill him. I wanted to talk to him. But he passed out."

"Why didn't you bring him back here?" yelled

Bolton, unable to restrain his anger. Mace turned his eyes on him and silenced him with a long appraising stare.

"There was little need. Chilson was simply a hired hand."

Bolton blew out his cheeks in fury. Shatford giggled. "Shee—it."

"Tell us what happened," Juarez said calmly.

There was a moment of silence after they absorbed the information.

Juarez sat up straight. "We know one thing. The wiretap on Chin-Sing-Ho was a feed. They knew we knew. Consequently Chin Sing-Ho is an andy."

Mace nodded. He knew that "andy" was short for "android," a term used in science to describe a robot made to resemble a human being. Therefore, an andy was a false man, a front, a screen.

"Perhaps the entire Sinotex Corporation is a false front," suggested Quinn softly.

Juarez nodded. "We've been wired to them for months now. It was the obvious conduit. However, if the S 176 caper was a set-up, we've got to begin ferreting out the chop."

"Chop" was a composite word made up of the first two letters of the words "chief operator," a computer word that referred to the main input operator of a computer amalgam.

"The chop could be anywhere," Mace said, leaning back. "Since Chin Sing-Ho is an andy, and since Sinotex is a false front, I'd think we have to look elsewhere entirely for our chop."

"Shee-it," said Shatford again.

"Talk, talk, talk," Bolton burst out. "I never heard so much bafflegab in my life. Instead of talking we should be out on the bricks, hitting the baddies."

Juarez smiled faintly. He resembled more than

42

ever the great stone face to which the peons prayed for rain.

"If we knew whom to hit, we would come out swinging, Danny." He hesitated. "I'm afraid this calls for skull sessions rather than bone-cracking."

Bolton fumed and took out his gold toothpick again.

"How do you think Chilson and his crew got the best of the rig guards?"

"I've been thinking about that," Mace responded quietly. "I told you that I heard Chilson and Rice talking about 'their man' on the platform. At the time I thought they referred to one man among the rigging crew who might be in their pay. Since all the men on the platform were in Chilson's pay, I realize now that they might have been shamming deliberately."

Juarez's eyez narrowed. He tapped the table in front of him with his fingernail. "Or he could have meant it, since at that point they figured they had you good."

Mace nodded. "Right. In which case he could have been referring to one of the men tied up in the storage bin."

"You say there were two of them?" Quinn asked.

"Yes. A heavy roustabout type and another man who looked as if he could take care of himself." Mace thought hard. "I'd put my money on the one who saw me."

"Why?"

"The other was out cold. I think he'd been creased on the head with some piece of equipment or tool. The man who was awake would be my guess."

"Description?" Juarez said, pulling out a lined pad from the center drawer of the table, uncapping his ballpoint.

Mace quickly spoke. "Typical rigger's face. Blunt,

hard. Blue eyes. Red nose. Probably a heavy drinker. Gray hair at the temples. Rest light brown. Rugged face. Wind-burned. Sun tanned. He was a stocky man. Heavily muscled. About forty-five or fifty. Hard-living type."

"Must be a million of them in Texas," muttered Juarez. "We'll put out a line on him anyway. I'll get this to Houston Police right away." He glanced over at Mace. "Do the police know about this yet?"

'Mace shrugged. "Probably not."

Juarez frowned. "I'd better contact Plato."

Mace knew that Plato was a member of H.P.D. who was also in the pay of the C.I.A.—with the knowledge at the top, and only at the top, that he was working both ends of a message conduit.

"Right. It was unfortunate that I had to dispose of all of them," Mace said softly. "It was the only way."

"Plato is safe."

"Good."

Benny opened the bottom drawer of the table/desk and lifted out a mini-phone of red plastic. Swiftly he punched out a number and waited.

"Plato?"

"Yes."

"Call me back on a safe line."

It took five minutes for Plato to get into a phone booth near H.P.D. headquarters and call back. Benny gave him the description Mace had supplied and hung up. No one had said anything in the room. Now Bolton leaned forward and smashed his fist on the table top in front of Benny Juarez. Slowly Juarez raised his head. "Is there something, Danny?"

Bolton's face was red. "We've been sitting around here in this god damned monk's cell for hours now, and all we've been doing is yakking. What in hell am

I here for? Me and Hank don't even belong here! We should be out guarding the oil rigs and the head offices. What in hell are we here for if you're going to sit on your ass and pick your nose?"

Mace stared him down. "There is a time for action and a time for thought."

Bolton simmered. "I've had about enough of this Confucious-say horseshit! Ever since you've been on the scene, China-boy, all we've gotten is trouble! I should have tailed those Red bastards to the rig myself!"

"Indeed," Mace interposed.

"I would of come back with somebody to shake the information loose from," Bolton went on. "What we got now? Nothing but an empty bag."

"I think not," Juarez observed blandly.

"I think so! There's been one hell of a lack of communication between the pod and S.S. ever since the death of that chink spy! I'm going to complain to the Institute."

"We have been given full clearance by the Institute," said Juarez reasonably. "The Petroleum Institute in fact came to us for help in trying to discover the reason for the presence of Charles Quon on the acreage of an Exxon field at the time of his death."

"You're giving us a shaft job," snapped Bolton. "I don't like it. You wait. I'll give them a blow-by-blow of this night's screw-up, and you see what'll happen!"

"Once we get the information we need from the Irishman on the rig, I think we'll be able to move," said Mace softly.

"How?"

Juarez said, "We've got him on the end of a string, Danny. First of all we find out who hired him. Then we trace back along the line and eventually discover the chop."

"Bullshit! You'll wind up with the andy again, right back where we started from."

"Maybe not," said Juarez.

"I'll tell you what I'd do if I had the authority," said Bolton belligerently.

Mace raised an eyebrow.

"I'd get me that andy and I'd waste the shit out of him."

"Yes," said Juarez maliciously, "and bring down the wrath of the Chinese Embassy in Washington on us. The man is a certified member in good standing of the Sinotex Oil Corporation. His papers are impeccable. We know the paper is just smoke. But all the same, legally, we wouldn't have a leg to stand on."

"I'll whiff the son of a bitch and ask questions later—"

"You'll do nothing of the sort!" snapped Juarez, his face like the facade of a cliff. "Be a little intelligent!"

"You're such a stickler for legality!" snorted Bolton, somewhat subdued nevertheless. "Why don't we just go in and arrest the son of a bitch! Lay the cards on the table. Show H.P.D. the tapes we've got. Give them a deposition on the chink's investigation. We'd have him dead to rights: entrapment."

Juarez shook his head. "Can you imagine what the District Attorney would do with that tape? Besides, Mace killed fifteen—"

"I don't believe he killed anybody!" said Bolton, "All this Kung Fu crap he's been giving us! I don't believe one man could kill fifteen men the way he says he did!"

Juarez smiled faintly. "You think Mace is not telling the truth?"

"I think he's pulling our legs!" snapped Bolton savagely, his face knotted in fury. "Anybody that

46

did what he said he did is some kind of genius! And that slant-eyed chinko don't look like no genius to me!"

"What you got to say about that?" Shatford continued, rising and standing beside Bolton.

"The wise man turns his back on the howling wind," said Mace without the flicker of an eye. "For he knows the wind blows on past and spends itself in the distance."

"Even if he had not killed fifteen men," Juarez said, endeavoring to reassert his authority. "Even if he hadn't, we would get nowhere with that tape of Chin Sing-Ho's. We'd be thrown out of the courts. And we'd be compromised, too."

Bolton sank back into his chair, momentarily frustrated but still seething and cursing under his breath.

The buzzer sounded. Juarez straightened and removed the red plastic mini-phone from the drawer. "Yes?"

Mace could hear the voice on the other end. "It's Pygmalion," said the voice. Pygmalion was a contract operative Juarez knew from previous deep-cover gigs. Directorate of Operations had any number of free-lance contract agents spread over the face of the globe who did constant traveling, keeping their eyes open for the Agency.

Mace knew that Pygmalion was a Chinese; he remembered having read his dossier. The man was a legitimate business man who had never been rolled up and was therefore totally clean and totally reliable.

"Sure," said Juarez. "What is it, Pygmalion?"

"I'm at Houston Intercontinental Airport," he said.

"Go on." Juarez flicked on the tape recorder attached to the mini-phone.

47

"I've just seen Major Fong."

Mace sat up. He tapped Juarez on the shoulder. "Ask him if he means Major Hsung Fong."

Juarez repeated the name in the phone.

"Yes," answered Pygmalion. "He's come in from Hong Kong. Must be on a phony passport or we'd have known at Langley."

Juarez nodded. "Is he staying in Houston?"

"From all I can gather, yes. His bags have been offloaded."

"What hotel?"

"No hotel. He was met by an individual."

"I.D.?"

"I do not know who the subject is. He is an American. Tall, freckled, brown hair, brown eyes, about thirty or so. A typical Yankee American. What you call the 'all-American type'."

Juarez smiled faintly. "Like me."

Pygmalion said, "They went out into the parking lot and got into a Cadillac."

"Description?"

"Two years old. Brown and cinnamon Fleetwood."

"Follow them."

"I would compromise myself," said Pygmalion. "I am with a companion. We are greeting arrivals from Hong Kong. In fact, I am possibly under suspicion at this moment. You must forgive me if I return to my companion."

"Roger, Pygmalion. Thanks for the information. Where can I reach you for confirmation of the Major's contact?"

"I shall call you tomorrow."

"Thank you."

Juarez hung up.

"What was that all about?" Bolton wanted to know.

The C.I.A. chief of station ignored the big man

48

and looked into Mace's eyes. "Who is Major Hsung Fong?"

Mace smiled faintly. "Major Fong is one of Red China's very best known trouble-shooters. When an undercover operation goes sour, Major Fong arrives to set it to rights."

"What operation?" wondered Benny.

"With the appearance of Major Fong, we must assume that whatever we have stumbled upon here in Houston is of international significance. The last time Major Fong was sent into an area to reconstruct a demolished Social Affairs Department cell, American intervention in the Vietnam War was the result. Major Fong is one of the Chairman's best.

CHAPTER FOUR

Angel McCready was no angel. He was no devil, either. He was somewhere in between—a rough and tumble roustabout who had always worked in the oil fields and who had lived by his fists and his wits through good times and bad.

As he faced Captain Dekker, Chief of Detectives of the Houston Police Department, in the small interrogation room, he felt the closest thing to fear he had ever experienced. He knew he had got in over his head, and he did not know how to get himself out.

Dekker sighed again, an impatient, explosive sigh that only hinted at the force of animosity and resentment that boiled beneath the surface. With his face that could have been made out of reinforced concrete, the pale agate eyes with their ice-cold stare, the bloodless lips as thin as strips of lemon citron, the cowcatcher jaw, the close cropped red hair that could have been that of a Nazi field marshall—Dekker was every inch the dedicated cop.

And Big Red McCready, the florid faced, heavy-bodied Irish slob who had laughed and drunk his way through life with the toughest of the tough men in the oil fields of Texas, was at the opposite pole from Dekker; they were two types fated never to commingle with anything but total opposites of views and purposes.

"Okay, McCready," Dekker grated. "You're in big trouble. Let's go over this just once more. And this time, give me something I can believe! We've got a total of fifteen men dead on an offshore oil rig, one survivor in the group, and two guards—McCready and Sanchez—trussed up in a storage shack all the time while one man—*one man*—whiffs the bunch of them!"

"It's the truth, Captain!"

Dekker stared belligerently into McCready's red-rimmed blue eyes a long moment, and then cursed flatly. "Let me have it again—from the top line."

"At about five o'clock Sanchez and me got in the company shuttlecraft and sailed out for S 176."

"That's an offshore oil rig owned by Gulf Oil?"

"Right, Captain."

"And the shuttlecraft is a 24-foot hydrofoil sea-craft used to carry riggers to and from the offshore platform?"

"You're telling the story, or am I, Captain?"

"And the S 176 is a rig that has been drilling oil for seven weeks?"

"Right."

"Okay. Is it the usual thing for you and Sanchez to be alone on the rig at night?"

"Sure. There's no need for a crew. Only when there's trouble. Tonight the weather was heavy, but it wasn't going to wreck the equipment no way. It was a routine guard detail. Me and Sanchez have been on that platform for three weeks now. We pull the detail together."

"You like Sanchez?"

McCready shrugged. "For a spik, he ain't so bad. He ain't no brain, but I don't mind to mingle with the masses some of the time." McCready was watching Dekker with gleaming eyes.

Dekker's mouth betrayed a flicker of amusement. "Go on, Big Red."

"Okay. We get out to the rig, and the riggers climb in the shuttlecraft, and they start for shore. The storm's beginning to come up, and me and Sanchez get a pack of cards and go into the storage shack to play a game or two."

"What game?"

"Draw, stud, spit in the ocean. Anything to pass away the time."

"Then what, McCready?"

"About seven-thirty I think I hear a noise on the platform. I go out and give her the double-o. But there's nothing. Only the rising storm. The wind whines through the steel rigging, and the rain starts beating on the deck like hail. Enough of that for me. I split for the shack and start playing again."

"Were you armed, McCready?"

"Sanchez and me carried pieces. Sure. Sanchez had a battered up old Mauser 7.6 mm from World War II. I think he stole it off a dead kraut during the Battle of the Bulge. Me, I had the old Colt .45 automatic I had when I was a drill sergeant at Quantico."

"I thought drill sergeants weren't armed."

"I was, Captain. And it was World War II. That was a war when everybody had a piece."

Dekker nodded. "Go on."

"To make a complicated story short, suddenly the lights go out in the shack and we're sitting in the dark."

"The rig was lighted?"

"Yeah. Night lights so you wouldn't stumble and

53

go off into the drink. Aircraft warning spots on the derrick and guy wires and the high crane. Craft lights on the ends of the platform to keep away seacraft. And lights in the storage shacks and the bins around the derrick. And night lights on the platforms for footing."

"What did you think made the lights go out?"

"Thought the fuse had been blowed out by a bolt of lightning or some damned thing."

"Would a bolt of lightning have blown the fuses?"

"Yeah. If the charge had penetrated the wiring anywhere down the line. Say there was a weak spot in the power line. Sure, the lightning would have grounded to the platform, since it is right in the sea. The line would have carried the surge of power to the fuse box and the lights would have blown. Actually, the box is loaded with circuit breakers, not fuses."

"And what did you do?"

"I got up and Sanchez and me started cussing. Sanchez told me to go to the box and reset the circuit breakers. I told Sanchez he could kiss my ass before I'd go change the fuses, that it was his turn, and we had a little friendly argument. Before I knew it somebody got behind me and pulled my piece out of my belt holster."

"Who was it?"

"Captain, it was pitch black. I don't know if it was a white man or a black man, an Eskimo or a Hottentot. Somebody grabbed my piece and shoved it in my back."

"Go on."

"I thought at first it was Sanchez funning me. I reached out to cuff him, but I heard a voice that wasn't Sanchez's say to me, 'You touch me again, you loudmouthed Mick, and I'll blow you away!'"

"Did you recognize the voice?"

"Hell no. Sanchez neither. Somebody relieved him of his gun, too. And we stood there like a couple of idiots in the dark. 'What is this?' I asked the guys who was patting me down to see if I had any blades hidden in my shoes. 'It's beddy-bye time,' said the guy frisking me. And with that he tapped me on the head. I saw stars and streaks of light.''

"And what happened to Sanchez?"

"Same damned thing," said McCready. "Now look, Captain—"

"Come on, come on. I want the rest of the story!"

McCready sulked. "All right. I come to. It's pitch dark and I can hear voices in the rain outside. By now the storm's blowing up a shit-hemorrhage. I find myself on the floor of the shack, my hands bound with some kind of heavy twine. I find out later it's nylon, good strong stuff. I try to yell out, but my mouth's taped shut. Only my eyes are open, and I can't see inside because there's no light in the shack. But I can see through the entrance that the work lights are on outside now."

"What did you actually see?"

"I couldn't make out much because I was trussed up like a steer and couldn't move past the pipes. We were in the shed where the drilling sections are kept. Okay, so I try to wriggle over to Sanchez, but he was out cold. I thought for a minute he was dead, but I wasn't able to tell at all. He didn't talk when I punched him so I guessed he was out cold."

"Didn't you begin to wonder what had happened to you and Sanchez, Big Red? Didn't you have a modicum of curiosity? Here you're tied up and strangers are cavorting all over the drill rig. Didn't you wonder what it was all about?"

"You're goddamned right I wondered, Captain! But what the hell could I do? I tried to eel over to the doorway, but the damned drill pipes were piled

55

in such a way that I couldn't get over them. I sweated and cursed to myself and tried to saw through the nylon, but that's like sucking up the ocean with an eyedropper."

Dekker sighed. "Go on. Get to the part where the —"

"I didn't see him come in. I was lying there, and Sanchez was still out cold, and I heard a noise. It wasn't much of a noise but it was close to. I could hear the sound of voices outside in the rain, and I knew the guys who had come in and taken us were out there probably pretending to be riggers on the platform. The noise I heard was close to me, very close. And *inside*. Away from the rain and the wind. You know. Close. And then suddenly a beam of light shot out in the dark, right in my eyes."

"What happened?"

"There was a pause, and the light moved slightly. I could see around the aura of it just a bit."

"What did you see?"

"I saw this long tall dude, Captain. He was standing there, looking down at me, with that itty-bitty pinpoint flashlight in his hand. He seemed stunned, really. I don't know what he might have expected, but he didn't expect me. I wondered what he was doing with the crowd of hijackers who had taken over the rig. I wondered what in hell was happening to me."

"Right. And what did the tall dude do?"

"He just stood there, and then he looked at Sanchez with the light, and I could see that they had worked over Sanchez a bit and had left him all the way out of it. I shivered when I saw that. I don't hold no big love for the little spik creep, but he's a pal and they shouldn't of done it to him."

"Did you see the tall dude good?"

"I seen enough of him."

"Tall? Six feet?"

"More. Six two probably. Thin."

"Go on. Did you see his face?"

"Yeah. He was dressed in a wetsuit, but the light from the small flash was funny. It tended to reflect back from me and I could see outlines of his face."

"What did he look like?"

"He looked—I know you're going to say I'm nuts, Captain—but he looked like a chink!"

"A Chinese?"

"A noodle-nibbler! A real live gook!"

Dekker considered a moment. "Go on. You say he went out of the shack?"

"Yeah. After giving me the once over he moved out into the deck and then the lights went on outside. I could hear voices, but I couldn't tell what they were saying. The rain was heavy and the wind howled through the steel shack."

"Then what?"

"I'm not clear on the sequence. But pretty soon there was one hell of a fight. I remember a bunch of gunshots. Not many, really. But I could hear screams and yelling and the sound of bodies hitting the deck hard. It didn't last too long. Pretty soon a couple of the guys came huddling into the shack to get out of the rain. I could hear them talking, but I couldn't hear what they said. Then there were some more shots and they ran out."

"Go on."

"Then—nothing. It was quiet again. Real quiet. The lights on the platform were burning, just enough to illuminate the well deck. And—well, finally I managed to get myself out of those damned nylon lines."

"You'd been working yourself loose all along?" Dekker asked with strained credulity.

"Yeah. And finally I got loose. Well. I went over to

Sanchez, but he was still lying there out cold. I untied him and removed the tape from his mouth. But he didn't stir. I could see a bloody knot the size of a goose egg on his head at the rear, and so I left him there. Then I went outside."

Dekker stared at McCready. "Go on."

"It was—it was like a battlefield after the battle's over. No one was alive, Captain! I didn't think so, at first. Later I found that one man who says his name is Chilson. I found him huddled off in the corner with a broken wrist and shattered leg. But before I found him I saw at least fifteen dead bodies lying around the steel deck. It was—it was monstrous. They had been beaten to death in every way imaginable."

"How do you account for that?"

McCready was at a loss. "I don't know. Chilson tell you anything?"

"Not a word. Doctor says he won't be able to talk for some time. And the hit he got, quite likely he won't remember a damned thing even if he does talk."

McCready rubbed his chin thoughtfully. "I bet it was that gook."

"Why do you say that?"

"He had something about him, a kind of an air, you know? A manner? He thought he was King Shit. I don't know if I make myself clear. I saw him in the dark there, standing like some shadow of doom. I could just feel his superiority. You get that sometimes with guys who are in love with themselves."

"You're sure he was Chinese?"

"Oh, hell yes. I've been in the Orient. Worked for Exxon for a couple years on a rig off Mindanao. He was a Chinese. I know by the shape of the bastard's cheeks and especially the eyes. And there was the way he stood there. The chinkos have this relaxed

58

easy way of standing. King Shit. It's the Confucious thing, you know. The Fu Manchu sneer."

"Yeah," said Dekker after a moment's silence. He stood up suddenly. "Okay, Big Red. Time's awasting. I'll have the statement typed up and you can sign it in the morning. I won't hold you any longer. I know you're beat to the socks."

"Yeah. It's been one hard night." He stood beside Dekker, towering over him. His voice lowered. "Those guys. You got any I.D. on them?"

"We're getting it," said Dekker crossly. "Why?"

McCready shivered. "I'd hate to of been one of them. Just lying there in my own life blood and shit, with nobody knowing or caring, with the rain beating down on me. Jesus."

Dekker grinned slightly. "I see."

McCready climbed in a cab outside Houston Police Department Headquarters on Riesner and instructed the driver to his home, a small cottage in a development just outside Houston proper. It was raining hard now, but not so hard as it had rained on the rig.

Once inside the house McCready went to the phone and dialed a number. The voice that answered was low-pitched and could have been disguised.

"Big Red McCready."

"Yeah?"

"I carried out my part of the bargain. Where's my money?"

"Everything went sour," snapped the voice. "Why didn't you help us out? All our guys are dead—except for one!"

"I did my gig. I let them tie me up. You told me to stay tied up so I couldn't identify your hit men."

"The boss don't like the way things turned out."

McCready turned red. "Listen here, you shithead!

I'm coming over there and beat that money out of you! You don't give me the runaround! I did my bit even if it didn't come down right."

"Don't try nothing funny, Big Red!" warned the voice.

"I'm coming over there right now, rain or no rain, and beat that ten thousand fucking golden eagles out of your hide, you mangy wop! Now get up that money!"

"Simmer down, Big Red!" said the voice softly. "I'll meet you halfway. You know Powell Road where it crosses Bowie Highway?"

"Yeah."

"Meet me there in half an hour."

Shortly, they both arrived at the intersection. A door slammed. McCready glanced out the window and wiated for the driver to approach him. Soon Nicky Grasso, or whatever his name was, bulked against the whipping rain by his side, tapping on the window. McCready grinned and rolled it down. Wind whipped in, almost drowning him in the driver's seat.

"Let me inside, you idiot!"

McCready opened the back door. Nicky fell inside, shaking water off himself.

"Where's the green?"

"Here," said Nicky, reaching into his jacket pocket.

McCready relaxed. He chuckled. In indulging himself for a moment's respite, he lost the last roll of the dice. The pistol barrel tapped McCready on the side of the head by the ear, and he went over in a dead faint.

Through the roaring in his ears, McCready seemed to be revolving in some kind of cyclone's eye. He could feel the heavy rain on his face. It was damned uncomfortable. He opened his eyes. The darkness spun about him. He was in his car, and the window was open. He could feel blood on his face.

Then he remembered Nicky and—

Enraged, McCready sat up in the seat, cursing to himself. He looked in the rearview mirror. The lights were there, about a block behind him. Nicky was waiting. Good. He'd get the slob!

For a split second McCready hesitated. Why had Nicky backed up the car? Why was he waiting for McCready? Would he gun him down when he came back to get the money? Why was Nicky being so cagy?

McCready glanced around. He saw the power line, the trees, and the lightning flashing above. For a moment he thought he saw a wire in the sky, but he could not be sure. What would a wire be doing in the sky?

The hell with that. I'll get the dirty little louse.

McCready opened the door, turned his head, looking back down the highway, and placed his left foot on the pavement of the highway. The pavement was running with water.

The power wire hanging down from the line far above—the line which Nicky Grasso had very skillfully and cautiously severed and allowed to drape on the top of Nicky's metal-topped car—the power wire instantly discharged its full potential of 20,000 volts through the metal roof, down the metal sides of the Pontiac, over the door frame and onto McCready's hand.

The burning fury of the high voltage instantly stopped McCready's heart forever, swelled his ribcage with cooked flesh, burned his abdomen, roasted his entrails in an instant, and then burned the thigh and leg and went through the shoe with such force that it threw it twenty feet out into the roadway.

From the car one block away Nicky Grasso watched with a white face.

"What a sad accident," he said.

61

CHAPTER FIVE

Danny Bolton sat in his plush, heavily decorated office in the Gulf Building on Rusk and Main, staring at the *Houston Post*. Sunlight blazed in over his shoulder from the hot blue Texas sky, which had not a cloud in it in spite of last night's big blow and wet.

With grunts of disbelief and snorts of dismay he perused and digested the article buried on page 37, thanks to the extensive lobbying efforts of the petroleum industry plants on the newspaper staff, about the deaths of fifteen men aboard the offshore oil rig S 176 the night before.

Survivors were listed as Lee Chilson, a man employed by the East Texas Demolitions Company, and Jaime Sanchez, a guard for Gulf Oil, owner of S 176. There was also mention of Angel McCready, who had been questioned by police from both Galveston and Houston.

Bolton shuddered and found it hard to breathe. So it was true! Exactly what the chinko had said was exactly what was written down in the paper. Someone had killed fifteen men on that platform while the storm raged and while the guards were tied up.

63

Police, the story went on to say, were already search-ing out leads on the supposed perpetrator or perpe-trators of the atrocities. An interrogated witness had described a man who might be the killer as an Oriental about six feet tall and in his twenties.

Bolton could not stifle the sudden gasp of breath that escaped from his lungs.

"Mace!" he cried. "It was the Kung Fu nut!"

At that moment the door opened and Hank Shat-ford came into Bolton's office. Freshly shaved and attired in tie and loose-fitting jacket, he looked ap-propriate to his surroundings—more appropriate than Bolton, actually, who still resembled the Staked Plains cattleman that his father had been.

Shatford was yawning and scratching his belly as he blinked at Bolton.

"Huh? What was that you said?"

Bolton shook the morning paper angrily. "I'm reading all about our Kung Fu expert! He's de-scribed as a genius. He must have had help. I don't believe it."

Shatford came over and grabbed up the paper. Bolton surrendered it with ill grace and reached for a packet of cigarettes on his desk. While Shatford scanned the front page of the paper, Bolton fumbled at the cigarettes and then threw them down. From his drawer he pulled a sack of Bull Durham tobacco and a small packet of brown cigarette papers. With infinite care he rolled a cigarette of his own, licked the side, pasted it flat, bent the end, and then put the other in his mouth.

On the desk in front of him sat a miniature plastic oil well mounted on a small metal base. It was a cig-arette lighter. Picking it up and flicking the wheel, Bolton got a flame applied to the end of the brown paper cigarette and began puffing on it. He set down the oil well lighter and stared at it with amusement.

"For Christ's sake!" Shatford blurted out.

"What, what?" Bolton asked irritably.

"Would you look at that? Angel McCready!"

"Yeah. The guard on the rig. We know who he is! What about him?" Bolton spoke in a guarded tone.

"You said you were going to question him. How can you do that when he's dead?"

"Who's dead?" Bolton squinted wearily. Shatford was not the brightest guy in the world, but he was getting dumber every day.

"Angel McCready!"

"He ain't dead. He's alive and kicking. What do you think it means that the police were interrogating him? Do you interrogate a dead man?"

"You bet you do," snapped Shatford. He handed the paper over to Bolton.

"Well?" Bolton said, hardly glancing at the columns of type.

Shatford came over and punched the paper with his forefinger. "Right god damn there!"

Bolton muttered, reading: "Stop the Press. Angel McCready, earlier questioned in regard to the deaths on board offshore rig S 176, was found dead in his car on Bowie Highway north of Houston early this morning. Apparently he had been the victim of a falling high tension wire. His body was removed to Star State Mortuary in Houston. McCready was an employee of Gulf Oil for ten years."

Shatford stood over Bolton. "Well?"

"I just read that he was all right," cried Bolton, "and now I'm reading he's been crisped!"

"The news flash came in late," Shatford explained slowly. "That's why it says 'Stop the Press.' Now the chink can't question McCready the way he wanted to. What's he going to do?"

Bolton straightened. "Hey, that's right."

"You don't look too down!" Shatford said with

surprise.

"I think the chink's a phony!"

"But what about the muscle man he claimed just come in from Red China?"

"I think that's all a plot the Kung Fu jerk made up to confuse the issue! I'll bet there ain't no such person!"

"Then what was the reason for that trouble on the rig last night?"

"There's something funny about that," Bolton declared. "I'll be damned if I'm not going to get to the bottom of this—no matter what it does to the chinko!"

"How can you get to the bottom of it?"

"I can talk to the cops, can't I? I'm a good friend of Captain Dekker, you know!"

"Dekker won't give you the time of day, Danny," laughed Shatford.

"He's a friend of mine! We both belong to the C.A.F.F.!"

Shatford shrugged. "What the hell has that got to do with anything?"

"The Concerned Americans For Freedom is a good organization of god-fearing, honest citizens! I've often talked to Captain Dekker there. He's one of the charter members."

Shatford made a face. "So?"

"Well, you got to give a little to get a little." Bolton's eyes gleamed. "What if I accidentally tipped off Captain Dekker that I know who that Oriental type is and where to find him?"

Shatford sat down slowly in the chair next to the wall and stared across the office at Bolton. The big Texan was slouched back, with the sunshime streaming in over his head. He was gazing at the ceiling in a self-satisfied way. Shatford could feel a cold knot in his stomach.

"You'd snitch on the chinko?"

"Who's snitching? I'm just letting slip a little information that I really didn't think was so damned secret. What's wrong with Mace being in Houston? Nothing. He was called here by the C.I.A. He's straight, ain't he? What's it to him or to Juarez that he's in Houston and if the cops know? And maybe in return for a lead on the guy Captain Dekker's looking for—the Kung Fu cat—I'll get a piece of background on Angel McCready. You can't tell me he didn't spill *something* interesting to Dekker before he got juiced."

Shatford leaned back. "You think McCready was snuffed?"

"Guys don't go driving around with high tension wires dropping on their cars every night of the week."

"Who totalled him?"

"The Reds, I guess. Maybe it's Chin Sing-Ho, the mangy little bastard at Sinotex. I'd like to put that guy in the slammer for the duration. You think he did it?"

Shatford shook his head. "You're the thinker, boss."

"I sure am." Bolton smiled contentedly. He reached for the phone and dialed a number. "Give me Captain Dekker, will you, Sergeant?"

Pygmalion's real name was John Lo. Although of Chinese birth he had been brought up in the United States, and had gone to college at Berkeley. After Harvard Business school, he had become a low-rung executive for Sumatro Oil Corporation, a company owned by Chinese and British.

John Lo had traveled to Peking in the first months of the detente between the People's Republic of

67

China and the United States, and there had established cordial relations with the Chinese half-owners of Sumatro. He had been instrumental in bringing to America Kam Wo Sung, the son of a very highly placed big wig in Mao Tse-tung's governing apparatus.

From that point on, John Lo and Kam Wo Sung had been almost inseparable companions in global travel, visiting all the operating fronts of Sumatro's oil drilling operation.

Unknown to Kam Wo Sung, at Berkeley John Lo had become an agent for the C.I.A. Later, at Harvard, he had gone underground and become a contract agent for the C.I.A. As such he reported only to the Hub at irregular intervals and only to local C.I.A. cells when instructed, unless he had special information to divulge, as he had now.

Because Kam Wo Sung had such important blood connections with Chairman Mao, John Lo's credentials were impeccable inasmuch as he was constantly with Kam Wo Sung. The two of them had the highest clearance available from China's S.A.D.

John Lo shifted uneasily in the chair beside the enormous motion picture projector in the booth of the Houston Paramount Theater. It was hot in the room with the big projector. An impassive Swede named Harvey Bergman was operating the machines, rewinding a reel just finished and loading the following reel onto the alternate machine. He did not look once at John Lo.

Bergman had been one of the C.I.A.'s safe house ops for ten years. This was one of the few times he had been called upon to help out. Bergman did not question his orders, he simply obeyed them. He wondered what a Chinese gentleman would be doing in the C.I.A., but he did not think to ask anyone about it.

It was then with some surprise that he opened the door a moment later to a rapid knock and found Victor Mace standing outside waiting to be let in.

"Mr. Bergman?" Mace said in his unaccented American voice, such a surprise in contrast to his very Oriental face.

Bergman nodded, trying not to let his mouth hang open. "Yeah?"

"I'm here to see Mr. Lo."

Bergman gestured with his head, and as Mace walked in, he closed the door tightly, and turned the key in the lock.

"Pygmalion?" said Mace.

"Yes. You are Mace?" John Lo said in Chinese.

Mace switched to Chinese. "I have brought a packet of pictures of agents of the People's Republic."

"Let me see them."

Mace took out the packet and Pygmalion began flipping through them.

"They are all Caucasians," Mace explained needlessly.

"So I see."

"You are looking for the man you saw with Major Fong," he said easily.

"Naturally."

"Do you see him?"

Pygmalion was shaking his head. Mace held his tongue as the C.I.A. man continued looking at the pictures carefully. He paused at one, studied it carefully, and passed on.

"May I see that one, please?" Mace asked.

Pygmalion handed Mace a picture of a freckle-faced young man wearing a slight smile. Mace turned over the picture and read the I.D.

"Clarence Hamilton," the pedigree read. "Six feet two inches. Hair brown. Eyes blue. Age, thirty-five."

69

"This isn't the man?" Mace asked.

"The man is too old."

"But he looks like him?"

"Somewhat." Pygmalion looked up. "There's *something* of similarity, that's all."

Mace nodded and waited patiently.

Pygmalion finished the packet and handed it back reluctantly. "Sorry."

Mace managed to hide his chagrin. "You're sure?"

Pygmalion nodded. As he watched Mace's hand putting the pictures in his jacket pocket, he snapped his fingers as an afterthought.

"You know. I'd almost forgotten. He had on a ring. It was a rather unusual ring. He was wearing it on the ring finger of his left hand. It had a fairly large red stone."

"A red stone?" Mace repeated, his voice rising in interest.

"I'm sure of it. Fire opal."

"A fire opal."

"Yes. It was in a gold setting."

"What was the shape of the stone?"

"That was what was so interesting. It was in the shape of a octagon."

"An eight-sided figure."

"Does that help?"

"Possibly." Mace smiled faintly. "If he doesn't simply take it off."

"But why should he?"

"He would if he knew he were spotted."

"He doesn't know," Pygmalion said. "At least he didn't tumble to me."

"I suppose you're going on to Britain now?" Mace said after a moment.

"Yes," said Pygmalion. "We have work to do in London."

"Good luck."

70

They shook hands. Then, exactly twenty-five minutes apart, the two of them left the Houston Paramount by the back alleyway.

Plato's real name was Francois Lafitte. He was a Cajun from the Louisiana Bayous who had spent most of his life in the French Quarter running a small bistro until he had been driven out of business by a combine of Miami Sicilians who moved in on the neighborhood and drove out all the original owners.

Lafitte had taken his family of four and established a new home in Houston. In revenge, he had joined the police force. Lafitte was not a simple man. He was a man of many complex twists and turns in his psyche, and he had never settled for playing only one role with any amount of interest or devotion.

During his days in the French Quarter bistro, he had moonlighted as a part time narcotics agent for the Treasury Department in Washington, and had been instrumental in breaking up three narc rings within a ten-year span.

When he had begun life anew in Houston, he had fallen in with Benny Juarez, and had suggested he might be able to do a good job for him at H.P.D., which like most police departments had an aversion to the C.I.A. The liaison was a needed thing. Juarez had telexed the Hub and had got immediate permission to take a shot at it.

Lafitte, code name Plato for the C.I.A., had worked his way up from uniformed patrolman to detective within a short time, and was one of the top men in the homicide bureau, under Chief of Detectives Captain Dekker.

The Police Commissioner had been apprised by

political connections in Washington, and had agreed not to interfere in the espionage operation.

It had taken no time at all after last night's call to identify the survivor from offshore rig S 176 as the man whom Captain Dekker had interrogated all by himself. Angel McCready.

Nor had it taken any time at all for the news of McCready's death by unknown causes to reach Plato's ears. Immediately he had telephoned the pod and told Juarez.

"Any other points of interest at the scene of the death?" Juarez asked.

"Somebody saw another car there just before the death of Angel McCready."

"What kind of car?"

"Couldn't tell. Nor did he see a number. You know, rainy night. Wind. Lots of scud in the air."

"You can't win them all."

"I'm trying to locate the tape of Captain Dekker's interrogation."

"Oh?"

"Yeah. Funny thing. It's 'filed' out of sight. It's the only one missing from two dozen made yesterday."

"Keep me posted."

"Will do."

"You think Captain Dekker may be in on this thing?"

"No. But I don't like that missing tape."

"Neither do I, amigo," said Juarez.

"A word of advice for you, Benny. Keep your Kung Fu Monk-Master out of sight for the time being."

A short silence. "What the hell do you know about *him*?"

"Angel McCready could have fingered him. I know that much about the interrogation. I heard one of our

72

men talking about it already."

Juarez whistled in dismay.

"That was one hell of a messy offshore rig," Plato said blandly. "Tell your boy to take it easy next time."

"Let me know what you find out about Angel Mc-Cready's death," Juarez said briefly.

Now Plato leaned back in his chair in the Detective Bureau and peered at the typewriter in front of him. He was writing up a routine report of a murder investigation from the day before. Actually he was keeping his eye out for Captain Dekker. Finally Dekker emerged from his office in his hat and coat. Plato glanced away and fumbled with the paper in the machine. Dekker waved a hand at the boys near the railing at the fore of the division room and went out into the hallway. Plato saw him standing at the elevator, waiting.

On impulse he grabbed up his own jacket from the back of the chair and slouched into it. He didn't wear a hat. It wasn't cold enough outside for a top-coat, in spite of the rain the night before. Plato straightened his tie, which was never very straight anyway, and slowly buttoned his jacket.

The elevator came and Dekker stepped inside.

Plato waved a had at Detective Fritz Keitel near the railing and pushed through the swinging door. Turning right, he hurried down the stairs in time to come out on the main floor just as Dekker was pushing his way out through the glass doors into the street.

Plato hung back. He saw Dekker glance up and down for a cab. Then, with a shrug, Dekker turned to the right and started walking along the sidewalk.

For three blocks Plato tailed Dekker. It was surprisingly easy and Plato knew Dekker hadn't made him. When it came to being a set-up, an expert seemed the easiest to take. As they said, get a thief to catch a thief. Set a tail to be tailed.

Sid's Spa was a small, ill-lighted bar on Rusk with a half dozen booths along one wall. There was a men's john at the far end and doors to a small kitchen. Besides that, there was only the long bar and the mirror with the glasses behind it.

From the sidewalk Plato could see Dekker inside. He was seated at a booth hunched forward with his back to the street. Someone was seated opposite him. Plato walked past, frowning. If he went inside, he would be spotted if Dekker happened to turn around. So? He could always say he had just stopped in for a beer.

And yet it was a dangerous business shadowing Dekker. Dekker would put two and two together if he saw him, and maybe ask an embarrassing question or two. If he pumped the guys in the Detective Bureau he would find out that Plato had been looking for the tape Dekker made on McCready.

The hell with it, Plato decided, I'll take a chance. Straightening his shoulders, he plunged into the darkness of Sid's Spa.

It was noisy, a juke box pulsating with country music, a half-dozen men seated at the bar talking in loud voices, the booths half filled. Plato slid into an empty two down from the end. He could see over Dekker's shoulder. The man opposite Dekker was not really visible enough for purposes of identification.

Plato ordered a Heinekens and happened to glance in the mirror past the boy in the neat white jacket as the boy turned to fill the order. He saw profiles of the men in the last booth, with Dekker facing his companion. Plato could see the man now.

For Christ's sake! Plato thought. It was Danny Bolton, the heavy eye who ran Petroleum Institute's

74

Security System! Plato sighed wearily. Rack up another zip for Francois Lafitte. He knew Dekker and Bolton were of a type. Dekker was a four-square law-and-order fuzz; and Bolton was four-square law-and-order private fuzz. It was not odd at all that they should know one another.

Idly Plato glanced about the bar and then the boy brought his chilled glass and set it down in front of him. Plato thanked him and poured the ice-cold suds into the glass and lifted it to his lips.

His eye strayed to the mirror once again. Bolton was leaning across the table toward Dekker. The two were engrossed in conversation. Without actually willing it, Plato read the words. He had learned to lipread in New Orleans when he had been working for the feds on the narc gig. He had not used his ability much lately because he had no need to. With wire taps and with amplifiers that could make the sound of a termite eating his lunch a hundred yards away sound like bulldozers bringing down a forest of redwoods, who needed to lipread?

What he saw made him forget his glass. It almost slipped from his fingers and crashed to the table top. Without moving his head, Plato put down the glass slowly and folded his hands lightly in front of him on the table.

The beer slowly lost its bounce as Plato slowly regained his. Who'd have thought it of Bolton?

CHAPTER SIX

Mace and Juarez were sitting on Juarez's patio. Mace was thinking of Major Hsung Fong. It was natural that he should be thinking of the S.A.D. trouble shooter, because his business in Houston had now to do exclusively with Major Fong. Yet his own mental training provided respite from constant worry over his principal enemy in Texas.

There had been a Major Fong involved in the Red Chinese Army during the massacre of refugees near Hong Kong about twenty-three years ago. Mace wondered if this one was the same man. The odds were against it. Yet, if this *was* the Major Fong he had read about . . .

Mace's father was an American—Victor George Mace—who had been in Communist China during the time of the Korean War. Mace's father had been a trader and businessman, at least it said so on his passport. Actually, he had been a global adventurer, who had found excitement and romance in Red China.

There he had found Su Li Nai, a Chinese girl living in abject terror under the Communists in a small village some miles from the Crown Colony of Hong Kong.

Mace married her there, and helped her escape to the British colony. And Mace's father had continued in his work to aid the escape of Chinese businessmen and their families who did not like to live under the government of Mao Tse-tung's People's Republic of China.

Two years after the marriage, Victor was born. It was less than a year later that his father went across the lines into Red China to bring out a group of thirteen refugees. One of the thirteen had been a traitor, planted by the Chinese Red Intelligence Service, not at that time called the Social Affairs Department.

Victor George Mace was murdered in an ambush the traitor had helped set up. But the twelve remaining escapees had managed to straggle in to Hong Kong, more dead than alive.

Two years later an almost inconsolable Su Li Nai had remarried. Victor's stepfather was Po Wa Hong, a kind and gentle man, who loved Victor as his own son.

It was Po who had sent Victor to a Shao Lin temple for his training and education. There Mace had learned the secret and deadly art of defense and attack—Kung Fu, the oldest of the fighting arts in the world, or what Westerners commonly called Chinese Karate. Actually, Westerners would be advised to call Karate Japanese Kung Fu, for the Chinese art ante-dated the Japanese version by many centuries.

At the Shao Lin temple, Mace learned also many other secret arts of defense—Karate, Aikido, Jukado, Savate. In addition, he was initiated into Tai Chi Chuang, Kiai-Jutsu, Tan-gun, Chon-ji, and Shao Lin boxing, as well as Kendo, Sumo, Yawara and all the other systems of attack or defense.

When he mastered these arts he would be, in the words of En Sheng, the *Tung-chia* of the Shao Lin temple, "A machine of destruction."

Mace could still recall his confusion when as a youth he had been told the various systems of defense and attack he would be required to learn.

"Master, I do not understand the need for attack and destruction," he said. "The principle of *Yin* and *Yang*, which I have begun to study, abhors all violence. Balance and harmony are the essence of life."

En Sheng had smiled inscrutably. "True. *Yin* and *Yang* are the beginning and the end of all things. *Yi* is the right way to do things. *Jen* is good will. With these four principles you will make decisions that are just, in making choices that will revolve around the principle of *Ju*, which means the non-resisting, and which is the Principle of Gentleness. With this principle you will study *Do*, which means Road. The Non-resisting Road is thus *Ju-Do*. Judo makes it possible for us to fight evil, for the Road—*Do*—must be cleared of all Evil."

"But Master, why must the Road be cleared of Evil? Why cannot a man bypass Evil?"

"The Road leads straight to the Truth. Evil tries to keep us from the Truth. As a *Tung-chia*, a Master, you must strike out at Evil wherever you find it. If you must maim to destroy Evil, you must maim. If you must kill to destroy evil, you must kill. Whatever you must do to neutralize Evil, you must do."

"But Master, how can a true disciple employ violence and still remain faithful to his vow of *Ju*, or Non-Resistance?"

"Evil is not an absolute, my son. It is a Relative Quality. The philosophy of *Fu-tza*, which you will also study, will explain the difference. Let us suggest a parallel. You are crossing a high chasm on a swaying bridge with a forest fire at your heels. There are fifteen people with you, who must reach the other side to safety, but the bridge will hold only ten. What would you do?"

"I would sacrifice five to save the ten."

"Exactly, my son. But why?"

"To do nothing and allow all fifteen to perish would be a worse evil than acting and killing five."

En Sheng nodded with satisfaction. "That is the reason when you are *Tung-chia* you will advance to destroy evil before it comes to you. You will be clearing the Road—*Do*—of evil obstacles so that the path to truth will be clear of that which is corrupt and defiling."

As Mace sat there now in the hammock in Benny Juarez's patio, he considered once again the implications of the fight on the offshore oil rig. He had acted then on the principle of *Fu-tza*. He had acted on instinct—on the instinct which was habit developed from years of training in defense and attack. He had not stopped to consider the implications of this man's attack or that man's defense, or even any one of those men's right to life.

The problem had become simply one of the removal of evil from the road on which Mace was traveling. The evil of the moment was the attempt to destroy him. If he had allowed the thugs on the rig to kill him, he would then have betrayed the lives of all those depending on his actions to save them. It was simply a matter of ridding the world of those who sought to stop him in his task at that moment.

Now the evil on the road of his life at that moment had been proved to be very real. Real enough to bring fifteen people to him to try to stop him. Therefore, something greater than the sabotage of the rig was in the works. The appearance of Major Fong on the scene had proved out the correctness of his almost subconscious decision.

Mace almost smiled. That had been bothering him, certainly. In spite of his years of training, he occasionally felt a vague regret at the death of a contender. But not for long. Evil was evil and must be banished, or the path would be bent.

And what was Major Fong here for?

Was Major Fong involved in the death of Mace's father?

If so—would Mace be exacting vengeance on him for the death of Victor George Mace? Would he be violating his oath of *Fu-tza* and indulging in personal retribution and ego-tripping?

Absolutely not.

The Kung Fu Principle of Justice, *Pi Tuh-t' l'tu*, demanded that Mace defend the rights of others. Actually, the Red Chinese soldiers who had killed his father were acting on strict orders. They were doing their duty. Now Mace was doing his duty. He was keeping the Chinese Reds from interfering with the rights of millions of people who might be affected by whatever chicanery Major-Fong was perpetrating here in Texas. Mace could not help the millions of Chinese in China from being subjected to slavery, or their brains subjected to washing, or their souls subjected to robotization. No. But he could see that slavery of that kind could not be spread about here in America.

As a Monk, Mace's first oath was to fight evil whenever and wherever the opportunity presented itself. And the American C.I.A. had presented him with that opportunity several times in the past, and was again giving him the chance to stop the Red Chinese in yet another attempt to subvert the American system.

The back door of the Juarez house opened and Benny Juarez's pretty wife Constancia appeared. She was in her thirties, a beautiful woman with a soft shapely body and pretty black eyes in a smiling face. She had three children aged thirteen, eleven, and nine; her body did not seem to have changed after producing them at all.

She kept house immaculately and tended each child as if he were her only one. Mace had not once seen her lose her temper with any of them. She was the natural wife and mother every man dreams of marrying.

"There is a phone call for you, Mr. Mace," she said in her totally American voice. If Mace did not know it, he would never have suspected she was born in Mexico City.

"Thank you," said Mace, and hurried toward the house. That would probably be Benny Juarez, or possibly Maury Quinn. No one else knew where he was. All communiques were screened through the pod.

Constancia smiled at him as he passed her and took up the phone from the wall of the kitchen.

"Mace."

"Hiyah, Mace," said a broadly-accented voice.

Mace recognized it instantly. It was Danny Bolton.

"Yes?" Mace asked, keeping his voice low.

"Listen, Mace. I got information on that guy you're looking for. Major Fong."

"Oh?" Mace's pulse quickened.

"Yeah. Look. I don't want to tell nobody else. You know how Benny is. I want you in on the kill, kid. I know this is a biggie for you. You being Chinese, too, and hating them Reds. So here's the scam. The guy who's hiding out the Major is going to be at the meeting of the Concerned Americans For Freedom tonight. You got that?"

"Yes."

"So be there. You look for me."

"How did you find out about this?"

"I got ways," said Bolton mysteriously. "Okay. You want facts, or you'll think I'm putting you on. Here it is. I belong to the C.A.F.F. myself. We're good Americans, Mace. And because we're good Americans, we're always on the lookout of people who might be trying to destroy our good system. Got that?"

"Yes."

"A good friend of mine in the C.A.F.F. happened to be at the airport the other night when Major Fong came in on the Hong Kong plane. This buddy saw the Major talking to a tall, lean, freckle-faced guy— just like that described to us at the pod."

"Go on," said Mace.

"He wouldn't have said nothing to me except that I was talking to him just this afternoon about our trouble with the Chinese. And he'd read the paper where Captain Dekker mentioned the massacre on the offshore rig. They had you pegged for that gig, but didn't know your name. And then he started talking about the flight from Hong Kong and said he knew the guy who'd met Major Fong."

"Did he identify the man?" Mace asked.

"He wouldn't tell me. He said he'd only tell you."

"What's the man's name?"

"Never mind his name. He's a roustabout who used to work with Texaco and is now a department store delivery man. He's going to be at the C.A.F.F. meeting tonight. You want to talk to him, be there and look for me."

"It's dangerous for me to be out in the streets," said Mace carefully. "I'm saying that only because Benny told me to say that."

"Are you listening to Benny, or are you anxious to get this creep that's hiding out the Major?"

"What time should I be there?" Mace asked.

"Nine o'clock sharp. Look. It's going to be at Legion Temple on Austin near Union Station. Take a cab."

"I'll be there," said Mace.

Once in the cab, Mace kept his eye out the rear window and finally picked out the tail car. It was a big brown Buick about five years old. He could not see who was driving it.

The drive in to town took about fifteen minutes, and when finally the cab let Mace off in front of Legion Hall it was exactly three minutes to nine.

In order to de-emphasize his Oriental appearance, Mace was wearing large wraparound sun shades, and an inconspicuous ensemble of tee shirt and slacks. He could have been Mexican, South American, or Oriental.

There was a large crowd filtering into the big Moorish-style building. Mace joined the group as they entered. He had just gained the center aisle and was looking over the front of the auditorium and the stage when he saw an arm waving at him from the right side of the floor.

It was Bolton, looking big and flamboyant in a bright red sports shirt, a purple scarf and high-riding doeskin slacks. He was eating an ice cream cone and calling to Mace loudly to attract his attention.

Mace crossed over to him.

Out of the corner of his eye he could see someone pushing through the crowd behind him, almost in his wake, but he could not make out who it was. He thought of the car which had been following him. Whoever it was had obviously got out of the car just behind Mace's cab.

"Where is your friend?" Mace asked as he came up to Bolton.

Danny Bolton grinned. He licked at his ice cream cone. "He'll be here in a second, Vic."

Mace glanced around. From the crowd a big man with a rock hard face and body to match shambled toward them.

"Mr. Mace, I'd like you to meet Bill Dekker," said Bolton.

Dekker removed his hand from his jacket pocket and showed Mace his service revolver.

"Detective Captain Dekker of the Houston Police Department, Mr. Mace," Dekker said with a leer. "You're under arrest on suspicion of homicide. You have the right to remain silent—"

At that moment there was a sudden eruption of shouting from the opposite end of the auditorium.

"Police!" a voice cried out.

"Look out!"

Two shots exploded, deafening everyone in the Temple. There was a flurry of excitement as people began rushing for the exits. Dekker froze and his head involuntarily turned as he craned his neck to make out the cause of the unexpected disorder.

Mace had been waiting for the diversion that he and Juarez had diagrammed. Informed by Plato of the deal between Bolton and Dekker, Juarez had met with Mace to discuss the set-up and how to escape it.

In order to allow Mace an instant's respite, and in order to make it seem to Dekker that the diversion was a fortuitous occurrence and not a leak, thus threatening Plato's cover in the police department, Juarez ordered Quinn and two contract ops to stake out in another part of the auditorium and wait until Dekker was reading Mace his rights before shouting for the police and shooting off the blanks that signalled an outburst of an unspecified nature. That diversion would enable Mace to split.

Juarez and Mace had visited Legion Temple in advance and had mapped out Mace's escape route. Then Mace had gone back to Juarez's place in Fairbanks to cab in to Legion Temple for the meet with Bolton and Bolton's alleged "informer."

Quinn and his stand-ins had seen Mace enter and had watched him approach Bolton. When Dekker pulled his piece and read Mace his rights, Quinn shouted and fired two shots in the air and set off the diversion.

The instant Dekker turned to spot Quinn's fireworks, Mace ran for the right aisle leading to the stage and the rear right exit, as diagrammed by Juarez and Mace earlier.

Bolton, confused at the noise, but instantly realizing the set up was coming unglued, waved his arm at Mace.

"Go after him, Captain!"

Dekker was confused. He hesitated and cursed, his face turning red. He could not move.

Bolton gave voice to a muffled cry of disgust and rage and lunged down the aisle after Mace, but years and years of good living and good eating and good wenching had added too much lard to his guts.

The Kung Fu Monk-Master was much too swift for Bolton and the load he carried. He knifed his way through the astonished members of the audience and was halfway to the far exit before he met unexpected opposition.

They were burly toughs, six of them, young and very experienced. As far as Mace could make out immediately, they came from nowhere. Mace remembered in the back of his mind that he had sensed rather than seen someone behind him, following him through the audience as he had made his way toward Bolton.

In the cab on the way in to town he had thought he was being tailed by Bolton to make sure he kept the rendezvous. Now Mace suspected that someone else had been following him in the Buick. He knew it wasn't Juarez and the C.I.A. And he suspected it was not H.P.D. Who then? Major Fong?

None were Chinese. Mace didn't know it, but the first man to have at him was a black belt Karate champion imported from Los Angeles for the job. His name was Jimmy White. He was the acting leader of the group of six.

White had followed Mace ever since the Kung Fu Monk-Master had entered the auditorium, as he had been instructed to do, keeping his five companions behind him. When he saw Mace confronted by Dekker, he had been puzzled and had not known what to do. But when Mace had taken flight at the unexpected diversion across the auditorium, White had called to his companions and they had spread out in the aisle down which Mace was rushing.

"*Hai!*" shouted White, taking a rugged stance and leaping at Mace with the straight thrust from the *hara* with the *Seiken-Choku-Zuki* aimed at Mace's solar plexus. An ordinary man would have crumpled under the impact and fallen to the floor, stunned and paralyzed from the stomach down.

Mace had seen the six men and had reasoned that the first one was about to launch an attack. When he saw the traditional Karate stance, he shifted position only slightly and came at Jimmy White with a paralyzing snap kick that landed just under his right armpit, beneath the extended arm that was delivering the *Seiken* blow to Mace's body. The snap kick with the full force of Mace's smashing leap behind it snapped two of the Karate champ's ribs and sent splintered bone fragments into the chest. White fell back unconscious and lay groaning in the aisle.

The second of the six was a black man from Oklahoma City named Bill Jackson. Jackson had been in the ring for some years, too, and now was a professional wrestler who made personal appearances at ringside before bouts.

Jackson lodged a smashing uppercut at Mace's jaw, but Mace, who had rebounded from Jimmy White to stand lightly on his feet and prepare for attack, saw the blow coming and deftly slid a lightning fast elbow smash at the pit of Jackson's stomach. Jackson was so heavy and his forward momentum was so great that he simply impaled himself on Mace's elbow, rupturing his stomach cavity and feeling the force of the blow all the way to his backbone. He sank to the floor, moaning and gurgling up blood from his ruined innards. He would survive, but would be out of action for months.

F.C. Pell was a slightly different breed of cat. Pell's specialty was sledgehammer blows with his head. He loved to butt his skull into his opponent's midsection, collapsing him and laying him out flat, at which moment Pell liked to jump on his victim to smash his ribs and break his legs.

Pell came at Mace from the right side. His shaven head was lowered and his neck muscles were tense and strong enough to break every bone in Mace's body.

With Jackson on the floor from the elbow job, Mace turned to see the battering ram of Pell's head coming at him. Mace bent his knees, holding his stance with perfect muscle tension and balance, and dealt Pell's throat a finger-stab *Nukite* blow to the thick neck from below as Pell hurtled toward him. The *Nukite* crushed the Adam's apple instantly. Then Mace's right foot came up with a *Kin-Geri* kick to the underside of Pell's crotch. The big bull-necked man was dead as he slid on the floor with his mouth erupting blood, his throat flooding with blood, and his genitals a mass of jelly.

The three other hired goons had backed away in three directions, determined to block the crazy Chinaman's hurried flight for the exit. Mace studied the three of them with instant comprehension. The one on the left, an ex-hood named Pinky Treyz, came at Mace with what he considered a good *Savate* kick to the groin.

With a quick and effective *Nami-Ashi* defense maneuver with the right leg, Mace neutralized the kick, stood aside, somewhat like a good bull fighter with a very close veronica, and hacked down with a hand-chop to Treyz's forearm with his right hand, and an uppercut to the elbow with an *Empi* snap from the left. Treyz's arm bones splintered like matchsticks and he screamed as he lost his balance and slid on his back into the wall. Mace helped him on with a bone-jarring *Heti'i* power kick to the top of the head.

The goon in the middle stormed in to deliver a Karate chop to the back of Mace's neck. His hand connected, and Mace rolled with the punch. Immediately he recovered, forcing his muscles and his psyche to regroup in a positive *chi* effort. Instantly he was clear-headed and alert, backing around, wheeling slightly, and clobbering the man called Hank Grogan with a Dragon Foot snap kick in the solar plexus. The ball of the foot and the heel slammed into Grogan's nerve centers, paralyzing him instantly and sending him crumpling to the ground. His abdominal wall collapsed and he was bleeding internally when they finally put him in the ambulance and sent him to Houston General. He recovered seven weeks later, but was on soft foods for the rest of his life.

As for Al Holtzman, the last of the six, he turned to run for the exit, making it a foot race with Mace. Holtzman figured that to be safe was to be sorry but alive. In the split second before turning to run, he had made a decision that the hundred dollars he was paid for the beating wasn't much anyway.

Mace reached down, caught his right ankle in a bone-cracking grip, pulled up hard, snapped the man's right knee, breaking the knee cap, and pitching Holtzman head first into the molding between the wall and the floor. Holtzman's skull was crushed by the fall, and he never even knew that he wouldn't miss the money he'd forfeited. He remained a vegetable for two years at Houston General, never coming out of the coma the fall produced.

"Stop him!" shouted Dekker's voice in the distance as Mace ripped open the exit door. A shot snapped out and a slug buried itself in the wall above Mace's head. Another followed, this one striking the corner of the door.

Mace ran through the narrow opening into the alleyway which he had measured and paced off with Juarez earlier. Mace was thinking clearly and quickly as he performed his muscular reactions to the attacks that had come at him in such rapid succession.

He had no idea who had mounted the attack, but he knew it was not Houston Police. Who then was it? The Reds? But how did they know he would be there? Mace thought of the car. Someone had followed him. Someone knew he was holed up at Benny Juarez's house.

The man who had met Major Fong?

Major Fong?

Decidedly so.

The cool night air closed in on him as the door

slammed behind him. He glanced down the alleyway toward the street. There were lights there. The alleyway continued to the rear and went around in back of the big hall. There was a parking lot beyond. He ran for it. At the end of the building suddenly two men appeared, both armed. "Stop!" shouted one of them. Instantly there was an orange slice of fire and the sound of a shot. Something whizzed by Mace's head. He pushed himself instinctively against the wall. He didn't like the lighted street.

At that moment the door through which he had come reopened and a woman appeared. In the half light he could not make her out. She seemed young.

"Come!" she called.

He held back, thinking quickly.

Another shot. He could see the two men racing for him, both firing. More shots.

He dodged back toward the door. The girl reached out her hand and gripped his, pulling him inside the auditorium with her. The fallen and screaming hired thugs were massed in a phalanx that kept the crowd at bay. Mace could see the infuriated Captain Dekker waving his gun in the air. He hesitated just as the girl pulled him around and led him down past the exit. They vanished instantly in a small descending corridor that wound down beneath the stage.

No one was there.

He could hear the shouts and especially Dekker's voice above all the others. "Get him! He's in the alleyway!"

In the confusion no one had seen him re-enter the building with the girl.

She led him through narrow corridors under the stage that were dimly lighted and then into a lighted dressing room that was deserted. It was painted green. There were long mirrors along the walls. In the light Mace got a good look at the girl.

She turned up her face to him and grinned like a pixie.

She was Chinese.

She was beautiful.

He was more shocked at the sight of her than he was at the sudden attack of the thugs.

She dragged him after her out the other end of the green room through a narrow door that had no sign on it, but which opened out of the building onto the parking lot.

She led him to a small red Toyota, unlocked it, and flicked on the keys.

They drove away in a cloud of exhaust. Now people were surging out through the exits of the auditorium, fanning out in all directions looking for Mace.

Above it all he could hear the cursing and scream of Detective Captain Dekker.

"I'm Moon," said the girl in a soft voice as they ran a signal and skidded around a sharp corner.

"Victor Mace."

"Moon Chu Lingdoo," she laughed.

They stared at one another with delight until the girl almost creamed the Toyota into the side of a building. From that moment on she paid attention to her driving. Mace looked out the back window. No one was following.

"You saved my life," Mace said softly.

"Not really. I just helped." Her nose wrinkled impishly.

"Where are we going?"

"To my pad, Mr. Mace," she said matter-of-factly.

CHAPTER SEVEN

Moon Chu Lingdoo lived in a small apartment in a new highrise in southwest Houston. It took only a few minutes to get there from Legion Temple on Austin. At the Museum of Fine Arts she turned off Fannin and wound around through several smaller streets until she pulled into an underground parking area beneath a glistening highrise with bright lights on in almost every room.

Mace kept glancing back through the rear window of the Toyota but could see no headlights that seemed to be following. The girl parked the car expertly and pulled out the key, gesturing to Mace to get out on his side and follow her.

In the noxious fumes of the underground parking area they made their way swiftly through the spaced cars to a small elevator in the corner where Moon punched the button impatiently.

Within moments they were whisked up to the fifth floor. Moon led him into a small, neatly kept, nicely decorated three-room apartment—living room, kitchen, bath, and bedroom. Mace stood in the living room, looking around as Moon quickly snapped the lock and put on the night chain. Then she turned to smile at him.

"Cautious girl," Mace said.

"It's not myself I'm worried about."

"Me?" Mace queried.

"Six people tried to kill you. Are you pretending it was an accident?"

Mace sighed. He headed for the doorway. "I didn't know it was going to be a question and answer session."

"You're a touchy guy."

"Just weary." Mace reached for the knob.

She stood between him and the door in as graceful an intercept as he had ever seen. Her face was inches from his. To his surprise he could feel his pulse quickening and his heart pounding. He tried to think of what En Sheng had told him about female attraction, but he could not remember. It was the first time in his life he had ever gone into a mental fog.

"Is it strange I should wonder what you were doing that would cause all those men to try to kill you?"

"They were sent there to rough me up," Mace said.

"They were killers." Moon's eyes were wide and dark. "And so are you."

Mace pushed at her to pass by, but she stood firm. "Let's leave it at that, Moon," he said in Chinese. "I'm grateful to you for your help, but I simply must leave."

She shook her head, took his hand and led him to the couch. For no reason that he understood he followed her with docility.

"Scotch? Bourbon? What will you have?"

He shook his head. "Tea, please. With lemon."

She threw back her head and laughed. "A disciple

of Mao Tse-tung?'' Her voice was laden with scorn.

"Nothing like that. I simply don't drink."

"Tea it is." Moon went quickly into the kitchen where he could hear her busting about.

He glanced around the small apartment with interest. There were Chinese paintings on the walls, interspaced with modern impressionist art studies. A stereo rig sat in the corner, with several record jacket covers exposed: Janis Joplin, The Rolling Stones, Joni Mitchell. A small magazine rack sat next to the couch, with *Newsweek, Broadcasting, Variety,* and *People* showing. Another pamphlet was exposed only partially, with the words, *KHOU-PBS-TV Annual Report* showing.

Through the half-open door he could see a small bedroom, as neat and elegant in its very modern look as the living room.

In spite of the neatness and the obvious good taste in the selection of the decor, Mace sensed an almost imperceptible sterility in the furnishings, as if Moon Chu Lingdoo might not be entirely open-minded and honest even with herself. Mace shrugged off the feeling. Who was actually totally honest with himself? Who was really completely uncomplicated?

"Then you haven't escaped me," a voice said from the doorway in a slightly mocking tone.

Mace glanced up quickly. "Of course not."

She brought the tea over and set it on a small folding table in front of the couch. She sat next to him and poured it, filling her own cup after his.

"Something you said disturbs me," Mace began as he sipped the tea and put the cup meticulously down.

She eyed him over the rim. "Oh?"

"I am not a killer. I am simply well-versed in defensive techniques."

"Like Chuang Fa, Aikido, Karate and Judo,"

smiled Moon.

Mace laughed. "These arts are not well known to most women."

"I am American, Mr. Mace. Not Oriental."

"Ah." Mace smiled. "Then why did you help me get away tonight?"

"I made a quick choice." Her eyes narrowed slightly as she seemed to probe within herself for her probable motivation. "It is a bad habit I have developed from working in the media. I make instant decisions. Often they are not the right ones."

"For my part, I am glad you did."

Her eyes were thoughtful. "I saw you surrounded and I watched you quickly go to work defending yourself. I suppose like all Americans I am for the underdog. I opted for you."

"In the People's Republic of China you would opt for the party, not for the person," Mace observed.

"You and I are not in the People's Republic," Moon said scornfully. "I am afraid I am hopelessly Americanized."

Mace looked into her eyes. She looked back into his. She was fearless, completely. There was absolutely no coyness about her. She had lost all that Oriental quality of demureness, that flirtatiousness so implicit and necessary in most Eastern women.

Mace did not know if he liked that about her or not. He thought perhaps that he did. She lowered her eyes and lifted her tea cup again. So did Mace. He found himself flushing at the nearness of her and at the images that passed through his mind as he looked at her again.

"How did you come to Houston?" she asked after a moment.

"By plane." Mace smiled faintly, knowing that he had deliberately misinterpreted her question.

She frowned. "No, I mean, for what reason did

you come to Houston?"

Mace laughed and found himself liking her more for her slight obtuseness than for any other quality about her.

"I am on a special assignment."

Her face displayed no expression at all. "Assignment?"

"I'm a magazine writer."

"Ah!"

"I write for *Time Magazine*." I am not on the staff, but I am what is called a stringer. That means that I report stories from the area in which I live. However, I am a roving stringer, and go where I think stories will break."

"And what story is breaking in Houston now?" Moon asked with insouciance.

"The biggest story of the century," said Mace with an unconscious grimace. "Oil."

"Oil?"

"The energy crisis."

"But the papers are full of it. What is the need for you to come here to study the problem? It exists everywhere."

"Houston is the center of the oil business in America." Mace looked sideways at the girl.

"But I don't understand what aspect of the 'story' you are researching."

"It is such an important story that the entire economy of the country is involved in oil. Energy is used for heating homes, for manufacturing goods, for many more things than just running cars."

Moon wrinkled her nose. "Okay. I believe."

"Up to the ninetten-seventies, the United States, Holland, and England controlled the total world energy trade. These international 'majors'—called the Seven Sisters in the trade—acted as a balance wheel between oil producing companies and oil consuming countries. The Seven Sisters discovered and produced oil in nearby and faroff lands and sold it largely in the industrial world. They dictated the price and the output of oil."

Moon sipped at her tea.

"A little over ten years ago, the countries that produced most of the oil for these Seven Sisters formed the Organization of Petroleum Exporting Countries." Mace ticked them off on his fingers. "Saudi Arabia. Kuwait. Libya. Qatar. United Arab Emirates. Iran. Algeria. Iraq. Ecuador. Venezuela. Indonesia. Nigeria. Gabon as an associate. These countries are now in control of the economy of America because five years ago Colonel Muammar el-Qadaffi of Libya forced through a 30 cent per barrel increase in the price of oil. He did it through sharp negotiating tactics against the oil companies operating in his own desert state.

"In 1973 the OPEC raised the price of oil. Since that time there has been a five-fold increase from $2 a barrel to $10.46, and government revenues in the oil producing states have soared from 91 cents a barrel to $10.14. These changes have not only squeezed U.S. oil company profits, but have also set in motion the enormous transfer of wealth from the rich nations to the poor."

"I think it's probably a good thing," Moon said slowly. "I'm no Communist, but I think the oil people have made too much money. Big fortunes have made certain men rich. Little people have been crushed. Others have been exploited."

"Granted," Mace said. "But there are important political power plays to be considered, too."

"Geopolitics?" Moon said.

"Yes. Because of their position in world trade, the big oil companies have traditionally acted as negotiators, non-political buffers between producer and consumer nations. But the growth of equity participation by OPEC and the across the board setting of prices have brought this role to an end."

"Okay, big lecture," said Moon. "What does it all prove? What kind of a story can you get out of this?"

Mace leaned back. "Look. Almost all the oil used in Western Europe and Japan—and a third of that consumed in the United States—is supplied from abroad! Don't you see what would happen if all that outside oil was suddenly cut off? Europe, Japan and America would be without a source of supply."

"We would have to get some other way to drive our cars," Moon smiled.

"You forget about the potential military threat." Mace got up and began to pace back and forth. "Don't you read your history? Don't you know that it was allied bombing of the Ploesti oil fields in Rumania that was the main reason for the demise of Hitler's war machine? Don't you realize that when his sources of oil were cut off, he was doomed?"

Moon nodded. "I think I see what you mean."

"There are two ways to bring a country to its knees. Send in your soldiers and take the country by force. Or cut off its ability to support itself. In other words, ruin it economically."

"And you think that could happen in the United States?"

"That's what I'm looking for in my story," said Mace. "That was what you were curious about, wasn't it?"

"But why are you in Houston?"

Mace thought rapidly. He opted for repetition. "It's the capital of the oil industry. What's happening in oil is happening here."

She laughed tinklingly. "You're a funny fellow.

Were you born in the United States?"

Mace shook his head. "Hong Kong."

"I thought you were much more Oriental than American. Did you grow up here?"

"No. I grew up—" Mace hesitated—"in China. I came over later."

"Your English is very good," said Moon thoughtfully.

"My mother spoke it."

"And your father?"

"My real father was American. He—died there. My stepfather was Chinese." That was enough of that. Mace stopped pacing and sat down. "I'll take another cup."

"The pot's empty. I'll make more." She got up and left the room.

Mace reached over and removed the corporate report of the Educational Public Broadcasting Service television station from the magazine rack and leafed through it. There were pages of financial breakdowns, showing operating budgets, profits, and funding from various governmental and private agencies.

He put the pamphlet back in the rack and glanced up to watch as Moon came in with the pot of tea. As he looked at her, something nagged at the back of his mind, but he could not put his finger on it.

"Here." She poured him a cup of tea. Then she sat down.

"And you," Mace said. "We've heard all about me. What about you?"

Moon shrugged gracefully, leaning back closer to Mace's shoulder. "I'm an American. I was born in San Francisco, and moved to Los Angeles when I was a child. I went to school in Los Angeles, and on to college there. When I had to get a job, I went to New York, thinking it would be better than the

Coast. But it wasn't. I did get a job there with Channel 13. That's a PBS station."

"Public Broadcasting," said Mace, remembering the corporate report.

"To make a long story short, I got a job with KHOU-TV in Houston about six months ago, and I've been here ever since."

"You like it here?"

"I love it!" Moon exclaimed. "Don't you?" As she spoke the words she realized that she had asked him a rather stupid question, considering what had just happened to him, and burst out laughing. "Well, I guess you don't! Not after those goons set upon you." Moon frowned. "You never did tell me who they were."

"When you do a story like this, Moon, you have to do a lot of investigation. You know, dig out things nobody wants you to know. So you run into people who don't want you around."

"And you ran into such a person?"

"More than one!" Mace scoffed.

"And those were the men at Legion Temple!"

Mace was thinking fast, winging it as he talked. He was telling her a fairy story as he was trying to think his way out of his own plight, trying, in essence, to pinpoint the source of the attack on him. How had those goons got onto his track? Were they connected with the police? Obviously not. Were they connected with the C.I.A.? Obviously not. Where had they come from?

"A few weeks ago a man was killed in a privately owned oil field not far from Houston. He was blown up by a tremendously powerful bomb on which he had been working. Nobody knows who he was and nobody knows who he was working for." Part of that was true, part of that was false. "I was nosing around, Moon. I must have stepped on some pretty

101

sensitive toes."

"And you think those hoods were sent out by the man who was blown up?"

"No. By the person who *hired* the man who was blown up."

"But what has this bomb death to do with your story?"

"Sabotage of any kind is a war weapon used by subversives the world over."

"But there's no war on."

"There's a cold war. I told you what would be the next step if the oil-producing nations could get the oil-consuming nations in a bind, didn't I?"

"Yes."

"We think they're rehearsing for a big move."

There was silence.

"Gee," said Moon.

Mace nodded. He sipped his tea.

"Excuse me," said Moon.

She rose and went into the bedroom, leaving the door slightly ajar. Mace frowned after her. He glanced once at the front door of the apartment, and then at the doorway into the kitchen. He could feel prickles along the back of his neck. Something was bothering him. He could not get his thoughts unscrambled. The presence of the girl . . .

He could feel the air about him move as if it were alive, and the scent of something subtle and entrancing caressing him. He looked up.

She wore an ankle-length house coat of brilliant green. With her coal-black hair in a bun on her head, and her yellowish-brown face painted spectacularly with bright-red lips, she looked like some kind of exotic plant bursting out of a green bud.

Mace's eyes slid to her waist.

The gown was split in the center, joined by a belt. But the belt was hanging loosely in its loops. He could see where the coat fell open at her navel. The shape of her naked breasts was clear to his eye, and so was the smooth curve of her hips below the navel. Her thighs glistened within the unconcealing folds of green.

"Mace," She looked down at him.

He stared into her eyes, finding it hard to keep his glance there. In fact, his eyes strayed to her body once again.

"I'm lonely," she continued.

Mace shrugged. "It's a human condition."

"I don't like American men." Moon sank into the couch next to Mace. The house coat fell open completely. She leaned on his shoulder. He could smell the scent of her body as it drifted up to his nostrils. She put her arm across his chest and touched his neck.

"I'm *half* American," said Mace defensively. His arm closed around her waist, inside the house coat which seemed to slide off her shoulders and crumple to the floor.

"'But you're half Chinese, *too*," Moon giggled low in her throat. "Which half?" She turned to face him and he felt her mouth press against his.

He lifted her quickly and carried her into the bedroom. She was biting the lobe of his right ear as he reached up and snapped off the bed light. Darkness closed down over them and the pile of Mace's clothes on the floor beside the bed.

He came awake suddenly.

It was pitch black in the darkned room. Almost instantly he realized where he was, remembered the pleasure with Moon Chu Lingdoo, began to stretch his satiated, exhausted limbs, and reached out a hand to touch her.

The smooth sensuous flesh—

—was not there.

He was alone in the bed. She was gone. Why? It was dark, not yet morning. He was—

Alone! There might be a purely natural reason for her leaving him, but, on the other hand, there might be a purely unnatural reason.

He tensed, rolling to one side quickly, sensing a stir of air, a shift in the placement of objects somewhere around him, a subtle movement.

As the reverberating racket of the gunshot echoed in the small bedroom and the slug smashed into the headboard with a splintering rasp, Mace moved quickly once again, hopping out of the bedclothes and onto the floor where he hunched naked trying to pierce the darkness of the room with his eyes.

The only blessing was that his assailant could see no better than he could. Another shot exploded in the small room, making his ears ring. And yet another. Three shots, all into the headboard, covering every portion of the bed where he might be, but where he wasn't.

The muzzle flashes pinpointed the position of the hit man—or woman, as the case might be. No sooner had the third gunshot sounded, with the long flash of exploding powder streaking across the dark of the room, than Mace leaped up—one step to the center of the bed, the second off the bed and onto the carpet beyond—to position himself within striking distance of the man with the gun.

He could see no better once there, but he struck out, first with his right foot in a *Mawashi Geri* roundhouse kick, to cover all the space around him. His heel connected with the man's middle, catching his left forearm and midsection in a stunning blow.

The man cried out in pain and backed away.

Mace shifted stance instantly and, using the

power of his spinning momentum, connected with a powerful *Ashi Zuki* stiff right handed stab at the gunman's neck. The blow severed the left carotid artery and the unseen assailant crumpled to the floor, the weapon he carried clattering to the carpet.

Instantly there was a fourth gunshot, the air about Mace's head reverberating with the sound. He could hear the slug whistle by his ear. It planted itself in the far wall. Mace knew that there was a second gunman hidden in the room, this one in the corner opposite to the site where the first man had fired his three shots. This one was a backup hit man, in case the first failed. Mace knew that whoever had sent these killers knew a great deal about him by now.

Mace ducked his head and flung himself forward along the floor, doing a quick front somersault and landing directly in front of the second gunman in a seated position. Then, with his hands curved and groping for the bulk of the man's legs, he found one, grabbed the lower leg just above the ankle with both hands, and, using his thigh muscles and back muscles, rose quickly and flipped the gunman into the air.

There was a cry of surprise. Another shot fired. This one hit the ceiling. There was a loud thump as the gunman struck the wall near which he had been standing, a cry of pain blurting out as his spine tore into the wall, and a sigh as he slid to the floor.

Again the gun roared. Mace reached for the weapon, judging its position from the muzzle flash. His hand touched the gunman's neck instead. Quickly he pinched the nerves in the throat, twisted around and smashed a deadly double-knuckle *Hiraken* punch into the Adam's apple. There was a gurgling sound as blood erupted into the man's throat.

A moment later the weapon hit the floor. Mace hard a sound from the closet only a split second before a knife blade sizzled by his ear and slammed into the door to the living room. Quickly he rolled over on his side and tried to line himself up with the closet door. He could remember exactly where it was, but in his gyrations he had turned somewhat from the position in which he had awakened, and he knew he was quite probably not facing the door directly.

He reached out and pulled the knife from the door and flung it far to the right, into the corner near where the window was situated. The steel blade clattered there.

Instantly there was movement from the closet. The door opened and a form jumped out, bounded across the bed in much the same manner Mace himself had for a spring-leap, and plunged into the corner to grapple the air.

Mace came up in a flying leap, crossed the intervening space, and dealt a sharp back-of-the-hand *Shuto Haishu Uchi* blow to the vague form he now saw in the dark. The third assailant rolled away from him. Mace had only struck his upper left arm, breaking the humerus bone. Whimpering, the third man turned around and faced Mace just as Mace struck with a left-foot attack from the air at the man's chest.

The blow broke four ribs and sent the man hurtling against the window sill. He grunted in pain, but kicked upward at Mace's crotch. The blow almost landed, but Mace had turned to the side to present less target to the man, even though it was pitch dark. He took the blow on the right thigh. Using the force of the blow to start a clockwise spin, Mace swung with his left arm in an *Age Empi* upward elbow whiplash blow which caught the antagonist on the right side of the jaw. The jaw bone shattered, driving bone splinters up into the brain.

106

He was screaming as he slowly fell to the floor, dead on impact.

Mace hit the floor.

He crawled around the bed and grabbed his clothes which were still lying exactly where he had cast them before climbing into the warm silken arms of the lovely, traitorous Moon Chu Lingdoo.

Quickly dressing, he rose and went to the closed door to the living room. He listened. There was no one there. Obviously, Moon would have left the apartment the moment she had let in these would-be killers.

And yet Mace did not like the idea of walking out into the living room and then into the outside corridor. If there were three killers inside the bedroom, there might well be one or two waiting outside, just in case the Kung Fu Monk-Master did manage to get by two guns and one knife.

The fourth man or men would be armed.

Mace turned quickly and made his way to the bedroom window. He pulled the inside blinds away from the glass and peered out. The casement windows were operated by a metal crank, opening outward as two vertical rectangles of glass. Looking down, Mace could see that he had five floors to go. Beneath the window was another set exactly like the ones to Moon's apartment. If he had a rope—

If wishes were horses, then beggars would ride. En Sheng had not said that, but it was a worthy thought nevertheless. Mace pondered.

He groped for the knife he had hurled into the corner, and found it. Gripping it carefully by the hilt, he made his way around the room to the spot where the first gunman had dropped after being torn apart by Mace. Near the man's right arm his gun lay. Mace quickly emptied the chamber, dropping the rounds into his pocket. There were four left. The weapon was a seven-round piece, a Colt Commando automatic. The rounds were .38 caliber super automatic.

Next Mace found the second assailant, who had died near the doorway to the living room. He swept the floor with his hand and located the second weapon. It was a revolver. Mace emptied the rounds into his pocket. These were Smith & Wesson .32 caliber longs. He guessed that the revolver would be a Colt or a Smith and Wesson, although he could not tell in the dark.

Now he paused in front of the door and waited. No slit of light showed under the door; Mace knew that the living room light was off. However, it was quite dangerous to move out into that new area unreconnoitered.

Time was becoming a factor now.

Those waiting outside, if there were any, would naturally begin to surmise by now, since their companions had not returned, that Mace had proved triumphant. They would be waiting for an enemy to appear. In the dark? Without a sound Mace opened the door. He pulled it back—it opened inwardly—and waited. Nothing. He moved quickly through the opening and pressed himself flat against the wall out past the doorway. Nothing.

He could see the slit of light under the outer door into the corridor. No other light than that showed anywhere. He could barely make out the shape of the door in the jamb, but he could see that the night latch had been lifted off. That was obviously to facilitate the entrance of the guards outside the door, should they be needed inside.

The ambush had been well-planned, Mace thought ruefully. First, disarm the victim in the arms of the girl. Second, isolate him in the bed. Third, attack him by one gunman. Fourth, back up that gunman with another. Fifth, back up the gunmen with a knife artist. Sixth, leave the living room invitingly open and lure the victim out into it. Seventh, kill him as he leaves the apartment.

Mace crept across the room with all the stealth his years of training could muster. He stood by the outer door breathing so shallowly he could not hear himself.

He listened.

Nothing.

Yet—there! He could hear movement outside. A man shifting his body. The particular manner in which the man had shifted his body told Mace that he had been extremely tense, as if waiting for something unpleasant to happen. Yes. Mace had been right. There was a man outside, waiting for Mace to appear.

Mace pondered. To open the door would be the greatest giveaway in the history of stealth. The knob would be moving right under the nose of the guard. The obvious thing to do would be to induce the guard to come into the apartment.

But the guard would not do that. He would wait.

Mace smiled. Quickly he pressed the inside lock shut and slipped the night latch on. The metallic sounds were quite loud in the silence all around.

Mace moved over to the far side of the room, standing just in the kitchenette doorway with the door almost closed. He waited patiently, counting. When he came to nineteen suddenly there was a splintering crash as somebody in the hall kicked in the locked door.

The door swung rapidly inward and banged against the wall. No one appeared in the doorway. Mace could see through into the dimly lit corridor. There was no one in sight.

Silence.

Mace saw the outline of the door frame alter slightly. He could see someone trying not to appear as he sidled next to the doorframe.

Then, slowly, a man appeared, holding a gun in his hand, peering into the darkened living room. Then, almost instantly, a hand snaked out from the other side of the open door and reached for the light switch.

The lights blazed on. Two shots fired, the slugs burying themselves in the wall opposite the door. There was no one in the doorway.

Mace waited. He clutched the knife in his hand, cocked over his shoulder in throwing position.

Now a man appeared in the doorway, glancing to his left and to the right, the automatic in his hand at the ready. He was a scar-faced individual, looking like a cast-off from the Mafia's execution arm.

He stood there a moment undecided.

"Nobody here," he said to another man in the hallway.

Mace pushed open the kitchenette door and stood in plain sight. The man cried out and lifted his Browning 9 mm automatic, firing instantly. Mace leaped to the side and threw the knife expertly. The knife sliced the man's gun wrist and the Browning fell to the floor, as did the man, clutching his bleeding wrist. Instantly the second gunman appeared firing at the place Mace had stood. Mace had circled the room swiftly and now chopped down on the gunman's hand with the barrel of the empty Colt automatic, shattering both radius and ulna. The man howled and dropped his gun. Mace heard a sound in the corridor and instantly pushed his weight against the door, sending it slamming shut. There was a third man out there! Bullets crashed through the panel of the door, tearing out chunks of wood.

The man with the cut wrist struggled to a sitting

110

position and grabbed his .44 Magnum with his left hand. Mace turned, kicked the gun away, and dealt a wide-side *Yoki Geri* kick to the flat of thug's skull. Then he reached quickly down and picked up the weapon, letting his empty Colt fall beside the still body. With the same gliding movement, Mace got the Browning 9 mm from the carpet and left the empty S. & W. there. As he came up, he unleashed a *Seiken Zuki* flat-knuckled fist blow to the chin of the gunman. The gunman went down. Mace flung the door to the corridor open. More shots burst out. Then, quite suddenly, a man hurtled through the door, his gun blazing.

Mace caught him in the neck with a flat heel-of-the-hand karate blow near the right ear. The man went down face-first, breaking his nose in the fall as he skidded forward.

The hall was now deserted.

Mace went out just as the gunman with the bleeding wrist rose and staggered to the door, aiming at Mace with his left hand and trying to fire the gun that had no bullets in it.

Mace turned and smiled.

He raised one of the guns he carried, the .44 Magnum, and the man turned white and fainted.

Mace threw the loaded weapons on the corridor carpet and punched the elevator button.

Instantly he raced down the corridor and ducked around the corner where the stairwell descended, then vanished noiselessly down the stairs.

CHAPTER EIGHT

In the Shao Lin Temple in China Victor Mace had spent a great deal of time studying the *Wu-hei Koti* system of memory, a method of sharpening the associational centers of the human mind to a point where a man had what could almost be considered a photographic memory.

"The system, my son," En Sheng had said, "is based upon the known fact that there are two parts or caves of the human brain: the active segment; and the inactive or storehouse segment.

"Images which pass in front of a man's eyes are imprinted on the brain instantaneously, as we know from a simple analysis of a moment's glance through a window. However, since a man must view the changing panorama of life from instant to instant, the human brain cleverly stores the images in large and convoluted recessed chambers of the mind.

"Most people assume that a moment's image is gone forever after it has passed from view. Nothing could be further from the truth. It is stored in the remote corners of the brain for recall when necessary.

"Consider a moment of great fear, a moment of great anguish, a moment of great elation—all these are recorded and can be recalled at will by even the most stupid of men. However, when not underlaid by emotional intensity, the everyday images of our lives fade into the interior caverns of the mind never, in most cases, to be seen again.

"What is the purpose of reviewing the image of brushing one's teeth, of shaving one's beard, or combing one's hair? Habit patterns simply recede as they should to the refuse pits of the mind. As one episode after another crowds out the preceding episode, discarded images descend into the mind's storage bins to be forgotten.

"However, it is a fact that all these images are there, to be referred to when requested by the brain centers. Because man habitually relegates to the darkness the images he does not at the moment want to savor or refer to, he begins to feel that once seen, an image is lost forever.

"We know by observation that the brain is the most complex organ of the human body. It is a fantastically complicated labyrinth of nerve synapses. When one wants to move his arm in a certain way, the brain responds, carrying impulses from one point of the brain to another until the message is composed; this message is then sent to the action endings in the outer body, and the arm moves in the way it is ordered to.

"In the other part of the brain are the storage synapses where the images are saved. With training, these images can be raised by the very same kind of associational procedure used by the mind to move the arm.

"It simply takes training of a sort that is known to the ancients and is studied by the masters of the Kung Fu. If it were a simple thing to recall any

114

moment of one's life, everyone could do it. It is not simple. Yet it is possible.

"The trick is to apply the combined efforts of *chi*, the psychic force within us all, and *teh*, the truth or virtue we all possess, to unlock the storage cells of the brain on command. With *chi* we dig deep within the thalamus and release the psychic powers within us to isolate and bring to life the image we want. With the help of *teh*, the universal force of truth, we bring these associational channels into operation, and the image is immediately there, restored to our minds."

"Yes, master. But how are these energies released to perform the act of memory?"

"Through two main channels, my son. Through the *Tu Mu*, a channel along the spinal column from the base of the spine, where a psychic center called *Wei Lu* is located, to a psychic center at the top of the head called *Ni Wan* and over the head to the upper lip. The other, *Jen Mu*, is a channel which passes down the front of the body to the genital region, *Huei Yin*. When we proceed, we will learn how to combine the force of meditation and the force of will to effect *Wu-hei Koti*."

Victor Mace recalled all this now as he sat in the C.I.A. pod above the World Travel Service offices on Congress Street.

With eyes closed and breath regulated in accordance with the practice of *Tai Chi Chuang*, Mace focused his attention on Moon Chu Lingdoo, from the moment he had met her. Like a motion picture film shown too fast, he reviewed his time with her in less than five seconds, and then at the end of that time centered his interest on one segment of that ribbon of memory.

He reviewed the frames of his memory until he held the corporate report in his hands—the Annual

115

Report of KHOU-TV. He leafed through the pamphlet and gazed at the pictures. He saw a picture he had glanced at on the couch when his mind had been on other things—on the charms of Moon Chu Lingdoo—but should have been on the subject at hand.

If he had been concentrating them, he would have isolated the face immediately. He had seen one quite like it within the past few hours. Now he concentrated on the photograph in the annual report and he saw five men seated at a conference table. His concentration fixed on the one to the right of the center.

It was a man dressed neatly but casually in a suit and tie. He had an ease of bearing which was obvious even though he was seated at the rather stiff conference table. He had a long, narrow face, with piercing eyes, and unruly windblown hair like pictures of Charles A. Lindbergh. There was just a hint of freckles in his face. His nose was long and straight, and his mouth wide and firm. The firm chin and high forehead completed the picture of an intelligent, determined, and forceful man.

Now, over this frozen image, Mace superimposed another picture. This was the picture that the C.I.A. roving agent, Pygmalion, or John Lo, had looked at twice before rejecting. It was the picture of a man named Clarence Hamilton. Six feet two. Hair brown. Eyes blue. Age thirty-five. "Too old," Pygmalion had said. The faces were different, but quite similar in structure. That is, the nose was the same, the eyes were about the same, the hair was the same type, the face itself was the same shape. The conversation with John Lo recurred to his mind:

"There's something of a similarity. That's all."

However, there was the kicker.

"You know," Pygmalion had said. "I'd almost forgotten. He had a ring . . . A fire opal. It was in a gold setting . . . in the shape of an octagon."

Mace focused his attention to the picture of the man. He was sitting at the table with his hands folded in front of him. The picture was quite clear and Mace tried to bring the hands into closer view. He could see the ring now, quite large, and the way the hands were folded brought out the shape of the inset stone. It was in the shape of an octagon. In the black and white photograph, of course, it was impossible to tell if the stone was a fire opal. The problem now was to get a positive I.D. on the man with the ring. If he could identify him, he might be able to procure a photograph and send it on to Pygmalion, to see if it was the man who had met Major Fong at Houston Intercontinental Airport.

There was a caption underneath the picture, which Mace now tried to read. ". . . assembled at a meeting of the Board of Directors in June. Pictured left to right . . . Thomas Galey, Director of Programming." If Mace was not totally mistaken, Tom Galey would be the immediate superior of the charming but unpredictable Moon Chu Lingdoo! There was no need to send a photo to Pygmalion. Galey was his man.

Benny Juarez slipped inside the room and approached Mace.

Mace came out of his deep concentration and smiled.

"Well?"

"Sit down, Benny," said Mace. "We're going to have a skull session that we should have had the day I came here."

Juarez nodded, running his fingers through his straight black hair. "I kind of figured."

By the time the C.I.A. chief of station had sat down at his desk, Mace was leaning back in his

117

chair and staring at the ceiling.

"It all started when Major Quon was found deca-pitated and torn to ribbons after an incendiary bomb of some kind had blown up at a point inside that Exxon refinery north of Houston."

"That's right. He was identified in fingerprint files by H.P.D. H.P.D. routinely sent the prints to the F.B.I. in Washington. It was there that Major Quon's tie-up with the Chinese People's Republic Intelligence Arm was established. Although F.B.I. wanted to bury the information, it got to C.I.A. Do-mestic ops phoned me immediately, scrambled the call, and I was told to trace back along the line to see how long Major Quon had been in Houston and to ascertain what he had been doing."

"Right. Then you went back over your voluminous tapes on Chin Sing-Ho and found only routine mat-ters."

"That's it. We know now that he's been an andy all along and—"

"Correction," Mace said. "We know that up to this point Chin Sing-Ho has been an andy."

"True. But in the new tapes, subsequent to the death of Major Quon, we suddenly came upon one that involved a man named Chilson and a man named Rice. The name Chilson rang a bell. Quinn flew to Washington and went through Army records there. He verified the fact that Chilson had been a demolitons expert during the Vietnam War. He was also an expert in incendiary bombs."

Mace nodded.

"And we found out that Rice was an underwater man, and had been involved in several offshore operations for one of the oil companies. Rice and Chilson were scheduled to meet at Bruce's Fishing Charter on Galveston Island. That's when D.O.D.

118

through the Hub suggested we contact you."

"I flew in the same day and made the meeting between Rice and Chilson and followed them out to S 176. It turned out to be a trap. And that was the end of a bad lead."

"Let's not go beyond that. I want to think about that whole caper a moment."

Mace sighed. "I've been concerned about it, too. There's something very subtle at work underneath. It's not just a plain trap, you know."

"I'm beginning to get that idea," Juarez said.

"If they wanted to trap me, they'd just take me. They knew I was coming. They knew where they could intercept me. They didn't do it. Why not?"

Juarez frowned. "Because they wanted you out on the rig?"

"No." Mace sat up. "Because they wanted to draw our attention *away* from something."

"Draw our attention away?"

"Yeah. Say I'd been killed, which is what was planned. You'd be doubly determined to go after Chilson and Rice, wouldn't you?"

"I suppose so."

"Therefore, it's quite probable that they didn't want you to think too clearly about something else. What else? Major Quon!"

Juarez blinked, his hooded black eyes coming alive. "I see what you mean. Here we go off chasing Chilson and Rice—"

"Because you think they were going to blow up an oil rig! You *forget* about Major Quon's death."

"But he was killed trying to blow up an oil well!"

"Yes. With an *incendiary* bomb."

"That's right. So?"

"The point is, they wanted us to forget about that, and to think about the offshore rigs."

"What you're saying is that the offshore rigs *aren't*

119

the prime target?" Juarez was trying to see through a haze of twisting options.

"I think I am," Mace said slowly. "So the entire caper was a feint. In addition to an attempt to zap me."

Juarez shrugged. "Then we concentrate on Major Quon again? We think about incendiary bombs and onshore wells?"

"Or installations," Mace said slowly. He shook his head. "We'll come back to this later. Let's go on to McCready."

"That's right. McCready was—or at least seems to be now—the bought-and-paid-for man on the rig who turned it over to the goons who were supposed to whiff you."

"And as soon as he was questioned by H.P.D., he had a sad accident."

They stared at one another.

"You think H.P.D. killed McCready?"

"No way," said Mace. "But somebody did."

"The chop?"

"Certainly. It had to be. But it was important that McCready be totalled. This leads me to believe that McCready was dealing with the man directly in control of the operation, or with an underling who would lead us to the chop."

"And who the hell was it?"

"Another dead end," muttered Mace. "Now we have this rather whimsical bit with Bolton and H.P.D."

Juarez sucked in his breath. "I've sent in a report to the Hub on Bolton. Got the reply back. Pretend it didn't happen, words to that effect. It's the oil lobby in Washington. I'm supposed to keep on working with him!"

"I'd do exactly the same thing if I was in charge. It's best we don't break off with Bolton. Let him hang there, thinking he's still clean. We do know for a fact that he did make a deal with Dekker of H.P.D. And the deal was to give me up to H.P.D. in return for the tapes on McCready. What did McCready say that was so dynamite?"

"Or did he say *anything*," Juarez observed with a stoney look on his Aztec face. "Is there some other reason?"

"Somebody thinks McCready spilled. And the tapes are still missing. Plato hasn't located them. That right?"

"Right."

"Now. Who double crossed Bolton and Dekker? I mean, who put that wrecking crew on me when I tried to split the Temple? It wasn't Dekker. He was waving his arms and trying to get a shot at me. Could it have been Bolton?"

Juarez looked disgusted. "I think so, frankly. He's got a deal cooking. He's sold you out. He's bound and determined to get you and deliver you, signed, sealed and delivered, to Dekker. So he hired six goons to stop you. Don't forget, Bolton knows you're a slippery type."

"Okay. I'll buy that. It could have been Bolton. He's probably got a lot of pressure on him from the Petroleum Institute. Somebody in their top echelon knows *something* is up, or Bolton wouldn't have been brought into this thing at all when Major Quon was found scattered over the prairie."

"Bolton must have figured McCready was the link. And if he could get the tapes away from Dekker, he could clear it up. Why couldn't Dekker?"

Mace took a deep breath. "No telling. Unless the petroleum people are in this themselves." The rest is cut and dried. The Chinese girl was following me. She'd been waiting outside your house, Benny. She made me way back somewhere. She 'saved' me to sucker me to her pad. And I really blew that one! She took me, hook, line, and sinker! I just about didn't get away."

"But you did," chuckled Juarez.

"And I did find out something that I wouldn't have found out if I hadn't been suckered." Mace smiled faintly.

"That's what you've been puzzling out?"

Mace nodded. "I met with John Lo, as I told you. He couldn't identify Major Fong's host at Intercontinental Airport. But he did pause once over one picture. I took a good look at that picture, Benny. And when I was sitting on the couch at Moon's pad, I was looking over an Annual Report from KHOU-TV where she works. And I saw a man who's a dead ringer for the picture that Pygmalion thought resembled his man. He's Tom Galey, Director of Programming for KHOV-TV."

Juarez stared. "He met Major Fong at Houston Intercontinental?"

"We can assume he did. Pygmalion is in London, or I'd call him and get him to take a look at this man's picture. I think he's the chop. What do we know about Galey?"

"Nothing," Juarez said, thinking back. "I'll turn it over to the Hub. Maybe they can cross pollinate with the F.B.I. and we can get a make on him. I'm not going to H.P.D. And I'm not going to Bolton."

"No, but don't cut Bolton out entirely. He's necessary. We can't lose a line to the oil people."

Juarez nodded. "That it, then?"

"More than that, Benny. We've got to move."

"Move? How?"

"We've got to get Galey and question him."

"Get Galey?" Juarez's hair fairly stood on end. "How?"

"Move in and take him," said Mace softly.

"Kidnap him?" Juarez's face turned almost pale.

"Kidnap is a rather frightening word for a simple operation like thrust and parry, thrust and question."

Juarez sat there blinking in bewilderment. "I can't authorize my men to work on that job, Vic! You know—"

"I didn't intend you should, Benny. I'll do it."

"By yourself?"

"I need help. You can get me help, I'm sure."

"Well, I suppose so . . ."

"I'll need an electronics man."

"Okay. I can get one. What else?"

"That's all I need."

"That's all?" cried Juarez.

"The wise man chooses the proper tool. The fool tries many and blames their quality.

Juarez shook his head in dismay.

"First we need to do some heavy recon. We've got to find out exactly where Galey lives, how he gets to work, and what the security measures in the building at KHOU-TV are. Can do?"

"Can do," said Juarez, still concerned that Mace needed only one man to work with him.

"I can't show my face, and won't until I take Galey. You get your men out right now, Benny. I want plans of those sites by tonight. We haven't got any time to waste."

Juarez opened the drawer and took out the red plastic telephone, punching away at the numbers before he set it on the desk in front of him.

Mace leaned back with a beatific smile on his face, his eyes closed.

"I think you're crazy, amigo," Juarez murmured.

"It is said, the sane man walks a straight line, the crazy man runs in circles. Yet which one wins the race when the finish line has never been determined?"

It was just after 9 p.m. when Benny Juarez came into the pod again to find Mace munching on a sandwich he had sent out for. Juarez was jubilant. He smacked a sheaf of papers down in front of Mace and tried not to crow.

"I got them, Vic!"

"Got what?" Mace pretended disinterest, although his eyes were narrowing in anticipation.

"The plans, Vic! I got a rundown on the security measures Galey made for his house out at Lake Houston—that's a suburb to the northeast of Houston—and also for his office in the General Jackson Building. That's right in the center of Houston on Travis and Clay."

"How does it look?" Mace asked, putting the remains of the sandwich aside and picking up one of the xeroxed sheets Juarez had dropped in front of him.

Juarez shrugged good-humoredly. "Not bad!"

Mace grinned. "How did you get these things?" He scanned the blueprints and spec sheets avidly.

"Both security layouts were put in by Alvaro Associates. Alvaro Associates is a Mafia controlled company we wired two years ago when the government was trying to get something on the Cuban drug connection in Galveston. We penetrated the organization with a man who was later betrayed by his mistress. That's how come we got the material. Our man put everything in the Alvaro safe on microfilm and we printed it up for the files. Before he got whiffed they had just finished the job on Galey's big ranch house on Lake Houston."

Mace whistled. "This looks very good. At least we know exactly what we're up against."

Juarez nodded with excitement. "Also, I've got a

rundown on every minute of Galey's average day. He's not married. He comes to the job in a Caddy driven by a chauffeur. It's got bullet proof windows and triple locks. Even if you ambushed him, you'd have a hell of a time getting at him.

"Also, he's protected from the moment he leaves the Lazy G Rancho—his spread—to the time he drives into the private parking lot under the General Jackson Building.

"Then he's whisked to the elevator by his armed chauffeur, who is really a bodyguard, and rises in a private elevator to the penthouse floor of the building. One elevator, express all the way. No other access to the floor. No stairs, no air conditioning vents without heavy screens or 24-hour alarms, no way. In fact, the windows are all made of five thicknesses of glass so nobody scales the roof and climbs down into his private offices."

"A guy like that must have some pretty dark secrets!" chuckled Mace.

"You bet! But he's cleaner than a hound's tooth, as they say in the boondocks. Not a spot on his record."

"What about the guards in the penthouse?"

"Full contingent," said Juarez, ticking them off on his fingers. "Double guard on the door in front of the elevator. At least a dozen guards on the floor, patrolling the office all the time. Permanent guard on the floor below to be sure no one penetrates the penthouse. The roof stairs are bolted shut, but a guard is there anyway. Guard at the entrance to the elevator in the basement. Two guards on the roof, just in case somebody wants to come down in a chopper."

"Wow! He's well protected."

"You bet your life he is."

"What about his employees like Moon Chu Lingdoo?"

"They're all triple checked for security. He's got only a handful of employees, anyway. The station programming is handled on his floor. The rest of the PBS station is run on the floor below him. The studios are two floors below, and the technical stuff is three floors down. Administration offices are four floors below—publicity, visitors information, all that kind of thing."

"What about the broadcast towers?" Mace asked suddenly.

"Yeah. Well, they're mounted on the roof of the building over Galey's penthouse office. And there's a guard there, who works with the roof guard. In fact, they work in tandem. There's a couple of maintenance shacks up on the roof, I suppose for the equipment connecting the studios with the broadcasting tower. But they're covered at all times."

Mace studied the xeroxes. "I can see all that here. Pretty tight security."

Juarez nodded gloomily.

"What about the—uh—Lazy G?"

Juarez groaned. "It's a nightmare. Electrified fence 12 feet high. Doberman pinschers patrolling at all hours. Four of the mangy things. Heat activated alarms on every square inch of the outer walls of the house. Triple locks on all doors. The windows are all sealed with alarms. If anyone comes in without the proper alarm-deactivating mechanism, the whole place rings like Quasimodo's bells."

Mace chuckled. "I suppose we could manage to get one of the deactivators, or fabricate one, and just walk in."

"Past those hungry Dobermans? Over that electrified fence? Without getting a gutload of buckshot —or worse?"

Mace shuffled through the sheets and tossed them

126

aside. "Okay. We got problems." He stared into space a moment. "By the way, what does 'Lazy G' mean?"

"It's a brand sign, that's all. An old hangover from the days when men had to brand their cattle for the big cattle drives."

"And to keep cattle from being rustled, as far as I have read about it," Mace interposed.

"That's right."

"But what does the Lazy in Lazy G *mean*?"

"Oh. It's simply a capital G written as if it were lying on its back. You know, lazy-like. It's a G on its side."

"I never knew that," Mace said wonderingly. "That's very interesting."

Juarez made a face. "If you go in for that kind of esoterica."

Mace unfolded a large sheet which showed the plans of the General Jackson Building. He stared at the details a moment or two and finally traced his finger along the elevator shaft.

"The private elevator is set off from the rest, isn't it?"

Juarez looked over his shoulder. "That's right. So you can't transfer from one of the normal shafts to that one. It's purposely isolated."

"The building was obviously designed for just that kind of private penthouse."

"Right. Public Broadcasting has always been there. But the penthouse was owned by H. L. Brant, the big oilman, when the building first opened. He blew his brains out five years ago, if you remember."

"I don't, but I'm sure there was a good reason for his so doing." Mace pondered. "Okay. The other elevator shafts are located on the opposite side of the building. And they don't go to the twenty-first floor. They only go to the twentieth."

Juarez nodded disinterestedly.

"In fact the roof of the building is uneven."

"That's right. I've seen it. You can walk out in the street now and look at it. Half the roof is twenty-one stories high, the other half is twenty stories high."

"What about the windows along the twenty-first floor?" Mace wondered, and leafed through the Xeroxes. Then he saw that the wall looking out over the roof of the other half of the building had no windows and no doors at all. "There aren't any windows along that wall."

"No," said Juarez. "So if you're thinking of breaking in there, forget it."

"Oh, I'm not thinking of breaking in there."

"What are you thinking of doing?" Juarez asked.

"I plan to emulate the wily hare who found himself encircled by seven ravenous wolves."

"What did the hare do?" Juarez asked.

"Let him who can speak to the animals ask."

Juarez threw his hands in the air in disgust. "In other words, I don't know *what* I'm going to do." Mace started laughing.

"What's so funny?" Juarez looked annoyed.

True brings low tar and low nicotine to the 100mm smoker.

True 100's.

100's Regular and 100's Menthol:
12 mg. "tar", 0.7 mg. nicotine,
av. per cigarette, by FTC method.

Warning: The Surgeon General Has Determined
That Cigarette Smoking Is Dangerous to Your Health.

True Menthol brings low tar and low nicotine to the 100mm smoker.

True Menthol 100's.

100's Regular and 100's Menthol:
12 mg. "tar", 0.7 mg. nicotine,
av. per cigarette, by FTC method.

© Lorillard 1975

CHAPTER NINE

There was sky and land, that was all: an empty sky with only the blindingly hot sun traveling swiftly to the westward on its way to dusty death in the rockly flat peaks in the distance; and a limitless, arid, uneventful wasteland stretching in all directions uninterrupted by the irregularity of flora or fauna to amuse the eye.

In the center somewhere near a point equidistant from all the far borders where the line of earth melded into the line of sky a spaghetti-like chain of pipes and silver storage tanks linked like glittering pearls on a string broke the monotony with glister and gleaming from the sun's broken and refracted rays.

It was a pendant of unimaginative beauty, a valuable necklace cast off into the sand by a deflorated virgin, left to remind the eye that saw it of hope and joy in the past which had turned to ashes and aridity and crumbling, disintegrating dust.

If the eye, bleared and teared from the blare of the sun, traveled around the circumference of the horizon carefully, it could make out a hot metallic blip reflecting the overhead sun—a metallic interruption on the horizon to the northeast of the sea of silvery pipe and tank. Upon closer examination, the metal giant would prove to be the hood of a large automobile, in which sat two individuals.

Air conditioning inside the large four-door brown and cinnamon Fleetwood poured cool air over the heads of its occupants. The purr of its special battery activated engine was the only sound in the car, or on the terrain, or in the air. The driver gripped a pair of powerful Zeiss binoculars to his eyes—ten-powers, with excellent visual acuity, coated with anti-glare sun-resistant filtration on the lens surfaces.

"I see it," said Galey. He moved the focusing knob for a moment or two, indulging his own idiosyncrasy of vision, and turned to the man in the seat with him. Major Fong stared impassively forward, his almond eyes squinted slightly against the glare of the dessert. The Cadillac's anti-glare windshield proved an admirable defense against the desert sunlight, but there was a great deal of heat wave interference between the Major and the field of producing wells which the two men were observing.

"You are sure the apparatus is set correctly?" the Major asked in a lilting, insolent tone.

"Yes," hissed Galey. He was getting god damned annoyed at the high-handed manner of the squint-eyed Neanderthal from Peking. In fact, he had entertained private thoughts about doing away with the son of a bitch in some clever and untraceable manner. However, he knew he was simply fantasizing.

If such a thing were to occur to Major Fong, there would be another Major Hong/Long/Song/Wong flying in at Houston Intercontinental Airport within hours to make his life miserable. He was trapped at this point; Tom Galley, one of the cleverest of his class at school, had finally outfoxed himself forever by becoming a high official of the formidable Social Affairs Department of the People's Republic of China.

The Major glanced down at the small black box on the seat between them. "Then," he intoned, "I suggest that you activate the transmitter and observe the results."

Galey nodded bitterly. He took the glasses down, squinted his eyes, and reached out to touch the square button on the black box. As his right hand pressed the activating mechanism his left lifted the glasses lightly to his eyes to watch.

Instantly a blinding flash erupted from the particular silver disk storage tank at which he had been gazing with such intensity. The flash was white and blue and orange, growing out to the ground like a tumbleweed, the outlines of its power curving up into the air where it abruptly mushroomed out, black smoke rolling upward and outward into the heavens.

Then, as the tumbleweed of flame and smoke separated itself from the bed of disks and thin piping on the desert terrain to roll up into the sky, a spear of blue-white flame spit out of the flat top of the same silver disk. The flame shot into the air, gradually widening, like the newly-lit jet of a gas unit on a stove. Black smoke began ascending from its apex.

A rumbling tremolo shuddered outside against the sealed windows of the Cadillac. The air seemed to vibrate around them even inside the car in the protection of its bullet-proof plate glass and its triple locked impregnability.

Major Fong was smiling, his yellow face wreathed in an obscene grimace of mirth and triumph. "Ah, ha!" he gurgled in his throat, overcome with demoniac joy. The sound reminded Galey of the throaty chuckle of a Japanese heavy in some old

131

Late Lake Show about World War II.

"Watch," said Galey. He kept the glasses on the producing oil field of scattered silver baubles. The high flame in the center suddenly leapt from its source—the first of the tiny disks to be blown up and ignited—to a second nearby. A blue-white flame lanced into the air, widening at its source. The second disk flamed, tore apart and burned brightly.

Again and again the magical proliferation occurred. Two, four, eight, sixteen, thirty-two—soon all the marvelous silver baubles in the sandy wasted landscape were burning, sending clouds of heat and gas and dissipated energy rolling up into the sky.

Major Fong clasped his hands in his lap like a prim, self-satisfied spinster teacher. "Excellent," he said, in Chinese. "You have proved to me that the device works. I will be very lavish in my praise when I write the General." With that the Chinese glanced aside at Galey, the veiled hate and distaste showing faintly in his black eyes.

Galey laid aside the glasses. He reached out for the key and turned on the engine. "We'd better get out of here. I don't think anybody'll be along for some time, but I don't want to be seen anywhere near this."

"Yes," hissed Major Fong, his eyes half closed with satiated excitement.

Galey glanced aside at him with contempt. Everybody else took the risks, and the Major rode in on the white charger through the gates of the city while the crowds applauded and the emperor threw him the key to the coffers.

The Caddy growled into life with the purring contentment of a large jungle cat and started off the wasteland to the nearby needle of pavement that cut the flatland in two.

"I am not a scientific man," Major Fong said as

132

he sat there with his head resting on the back of the seat, his eyes closed dreamily. "Do you understand how this incendiary device works?"

Galey considered saying no, but then decided against that. If, for some reason, someone in Peking happened to pull out one of his previous reports, he would see that Galey did indeed know pretty well how Major Quon's multiplex incendiary bomb unit worked.

"It's relatively simple, once you know the formula for the explosive. The average incendiary bomb blows up and spreads flaming jelly all around. The jelly sticks to anything flammable—which is actually almost everything—and burns that too. The problem is, the amount of flaming jelly which is ejected by the explosion of the bomb pretty much limits the area in which the fire can be calculated to burn.

"Major Quon redesigned the properties of the incendiary ingredient, and changed it from a jelly to a chemical mixture which continually regenerates itself as it combines with oxygen. I'm not putting this very well, but the point is, what you just saw pretty well explains it. The incendiary bomb goes off. The object to which it is attached is set on fire. The heat of that fire causes the inert high-heat-resistant secondary chemical in the bomb to expand rapidly into a hot spray as it is mixed with oxygen. The spray lights on a nearby object and immediately sets it on fire at a tremendously high temperature. That object in turn burns and the secondary chemical once again expands rapidly as it is united with oxygen and stimulated by heat. It then sets on fire a third object, and so on."

"Formidable!"

"Just so," said Galey.

"How did you attach the bomb to the tank just

133

now?'' Major Fong asked.

Galey glanced aside at the Chinese and pondered a moment. Well, why not? The old bastard would know sooner or later anyway. And if he didn't, an examination of the unit would show exactly how it was done. No use making a big thing out of it.

"It's a limpet mine principle," he said. "You just attach it to something metallic and it sticks right there. It's black and innocent looking. Nobody will notice it around a petroleum refinery installation or producing field."

Major Fong smiled maliciously. "Indeed not." He sighed and closed his eyes once again. His fingers began playing with one another in his lap. He seemed to be humming something musical and satisfying to himself in his imagination. "Beautiful," he muttered. "Now that we have seen the unit itself in action, perhaps you would be so good as to allow me to see the remainder of the plan of operation."

Galey shrugged. "Why not? It's set to go anytime you get the word from Peking."

Major Fong nodded. His eyes opened and slid down to the little black box on the seat between them. "Your technology is absolutely fantastic, Captain Galey." Galey almost started. It was the first time the Major had addressed him by his rank in the S.A.D. since he had come to Houston. "You must explain to me how the pressing of that button made the bomb blow up at the producing well."

"It's a radio transmitter," said Galey, barely disguising his contempt. "The black box is a battery transmitter. It transmits a signal through the air to the bomb unit. The signal is received by a tiny transistor radio-receiver unit in the bomb. When the current flows in the receiver in the bomb at the reception of the signal, the primer in the bomb is ignited. The bomb explodes and the fiery incendiary mix begins to burn."

Major Fong nodded thoughtfully. "And how far does the little black box reach with its signal?"

"Probably three or four miles."

"Then I do not understand how we will be able to accomplish our mission on the scale at which it has been planned."

There was silence for a moment.

"Major, just leave it to me. You're not the scientist Major Quon was. He had that part all set up before he even began work on the incendiary unit. In fact, that part was in the works weeks ago."

Major Fong frowned. "I don't want to appear obtuse, but I do not quite understand. If your signal will only travel four miles—"

"When we get back to the spread I'll show you," Galey said abruptly. He glanced in the rearview mirror and was happy to see that they had come down off the barren plateau and were now almost out of sight of the black clouds of smoke rising in the air. When he glanced at the roadway in front of him he could see a helicopter in the distance, with the sun glinting on its rotors. Someone had apparently spotted the burning oil field.

Ahead there was a group of gas stations. He decided to pull in and wait for the chopper to pass over. It wouldn't do to have the pilot spot him on the highway coming away from the field. As for the gas station attendants, if they got curious he could always buy them off. Chewing thoughtfully on the inside of his lower lip, Galey decelerated and glanced once again into the sky.

"Low on gas," he told the Major. "Got to fill up."

Major Fong smiled. He said nothing. He looked happy. He should look happy, Galey snorted to himself. He'd get a promotion out of this. What would Galey get? A promotion, too. He's be head of

135

Counter Intelligence in the United States of China. Somehow it didn't really ring right to him—the United States of China! But he'd made the decision a long time ago, and it was not time to have second thoughts.

Right on, Chairman Mao!

He pulled up to the gas tank. As he did so he thought ironically that the whole world struggle today was over the simple fluid in that pump: gasoline, petroleum, natural gas. Energy.

Power, by god!

The power to tear apart the country that even General Robert E. Lee couldn't break in two.

And here old Tom Galey was doing it almost single-handed.

With the help of Major Quon's ghost, of course.

"Fill it up, kid," he told the redheaded youth who came out of the station grinning at him.

Fill it up with power, kid.

Power to Tom Galey.

Moon Chu Lingdoo sat desolately on the bed in the large bedroom of Tom Galey's Lazy G ranch house with her legs spread wide and her head hanging down. She was itching to have a shower and feeling really raunchy in the nice new pants suit she was wearing.

Shuddering, she rose to her feet and went over to the window. Looking out she could see the bright Texas day, the beautiful garden which had just been watered by the freako mute black who tended the plants, and the twelve-foot-high electrified fence beyond. Past that there were smaller houses and a lot of low-growing trees and wild bush stuff that bred so well in Texas's weird soil.

If only she could get out into the sun, maybe she

would have a chance to split the Galey place. But it was obvious that the window was sealed tight; breaking it would only activate not only the electric alarm system but would immediately send burning rays across the open space. At least that was what Tom Galey said, and she had no reason to doubt his word.

It was her own damned fault, she decided. She never should have let Galey take her away after that fiasco with the Kung Fu Monk-Master. But it wasn't Galey who frightened her; after all, she had worked for him for six months or so. It was that really sick Mao Tse-tung type Major Fong who made her want to heave her guts.

Wow!

Galey had lured her to the ranch house, no question about that. He had appeared, all innocent and shining like a school kid on the way to eight o'clock mass, just after she had phoned him and told him the Kung Fu creep had got away, leaving six victims dead or out cold.

Quickly he had warned her to tell no one and to wait for him; he would hide her out. There would be police and all that, later. Of course, she knew that. There was no way for her to clean up the bodies. Besides that, there had been plenty of people who had heard the shots. Luckily no one had intervened; everyone was afraid of getting involved. Swinging Houston was just like swinging New York. Nobody—*but nobody,* wanted an inch-and-a-half of trouble.

So like a real jerk she had come with Galey in his big brown and cinnamon Caddy to the ranch. She had heard about the place—what a beautiful thing it was—but it was beyond her wildest expectations. Beautiful lake view. Beautiful gardens. Beautiful rambling house. Elegant furniture.

But she hadn't counted on Major Fong.

That creep had come into her boss's big living room shortly after she had arrived, while she and Mr. Galey were drinking coffee and chatting merrily away, and begun to—

Well . . .

"I am told you have failed in your mission, Miss Lingdoo!" the Major intoned in his slightly lisping, almost academic Chinese.

"Yes sir," Moon replied. "It won't happen again. Everything worked splendidly until your—"

"*Again*! There will be no again! You are through, Miss Lingdoo! Through! What is this misconception about *again*? There is room for no mistakes in the People's Republic of China!"

Moon stared. "But, sir—" For some reason she felt like saying "sir" to the creep, although she felt her flesh crawl when she looked at him. He was repulsive and frightening. The hell with him!

"What possible good are you to us now, young lady?" Major Fong whined. "I fear you are simply an albatross around our neck. Yes! That is a good phrase. An albatross around our neck." He giggled. "How could you help us trap that wily Kung Fu ace again? He knows you now. Of what earthly good are you? You have failed in your mission to kill him. You are finished, Miss Lingdoo."

Galey intervened. "Major Fong, let's not be hasty. I've told Moon that she can hide out here until we arrange for another post for her. After all—"

"Another post for her, indeed!" snarled Major Fong. "If you can't find a place to get rid of her here, we'll send her on to Peking! The Chairman will find a place for her—sweeping the streets of dung in the early morning hours!"

"What is this?" yelled Moon, getting excited. "You can't be serious! I'm a qualified member of the S.A.D. You can't boss me around—"

"I'm your superior, Miss Lingdoo," snapped Major Fong, his face mottled like an old tire. He leaned closer to her and breathed his almondy breath on her. "You're no better to us now than a worn-out whore or a courtesan with the clap! Now go out and kill yourself if you wish. It would certainly save us making a mess on the rug."

Moon leaped to her feet and jumped at the man, stabbing out at him with her fingernails, going for his eyes. "You dirty old man! You're no better than any of those rice bowl beggars in Peking! I'm not going there!"

Major Fong backhanded her in the face and she sprawled across the couch. She was sobbing when she finally got herself to her feet.

Galey was standing there between her and the Major. "Moon!" he said distinctly. "Go to your room."

"Let me handle her," said Major Fong in a low deadly voice. "I'll turn her inside out like a glove."

"Shut up," snapped Galey. "Moon. Go to the bedroom I showed you. The Major and I have a trip to make today. I'll see you later."

Moon wiped her eyes. She was breathing heavily. Her hair was a mess. She licked her lip and tasted blood. "You god damned son of a bitch," she said to the Major over Galey's shoulder. "You come near me and I'll kick you in the crotch."

The Major's eyes blazed. "Woman—"

"That's enough," Galey said to Moon, taking her by the shoulders and pushing her out of the room. "Get out of here. I'll handle him," he whispered.

And she reeled on down the hallway to the room he had shown her. Once she was inside, the door had been bolted from the outside. She could hear a man out there. He was breathing heavily, wheezing kind of, and smoking a vile-smelling cigarette. It smelled like very inferior pot. Mexican grass maybe. Rotten.

The Caddy left at about noon time. Moon went to the door and listened. She could hear the guard wheezing.

"Hey," she said.

"Yeah?" It was an American voice, not Chinese. Her spirits rose.

"You work for Tom?"

"Mr. Galey? Yeah." The dude had a New York accent. Good!

"What's your name?"

"Nicky."

"Hi, Nickey."

"Hey, kitten. They told me not to talk."

"So?" Moon said, "Can you give me a cigarette? I'm dying for a smoke."

"No," said Nicky.

"My name is Moon. Ain't that a kick?"

"Funny. You a spik?"

"I'm Chinese," said Moon, trying not to bridle. "But I'm an American."

"Mr. Galey said not to talk to you."

"Yeah? He's jealous. I got something for you, Nicky."

Silence. "Yeah?" Nicky was interested. She could feel his interest even through the closed door. "What you got?"

She chuckled. "Listen. I don't want to split or anything stupid like that. I want to stay here. Mr. Galey is good to me. But I want a cigarette."

"Uh huh."

"I could give you something good for a cigarette."

"What good?" Nicky was definitely interested. She could hear the rising quality of his voice.

"Plenty good, Nicky. You ask Mr. Galey some time. You see if I'm not plenty good."

"He'd kill me."

"Who'd tell him? I wouldn't tell him. You wouldn't tell him. Who'd tell him, Nicky? You know he's gone for the day."

"Yeah," said Nick. There was a rustling sound. The door knob turned and the door opened.

He stood in the small opening, a short, mean looking, scar-faced Sicilian thug with a cast to one eye and a pair of broken front teeth. She shuffled, but managed to stroke her hips with her hands in a seductive manner. She wished to hell she had been wearing a skirt and blouse. The damned pants suit wasn't too terrifically sexy.

He handed in a ragged cigarette that was unlighted, but looked filthy nevertheless. She took it and leaned back so he had to poke his head further in. "Give me a light."

He got a lighter in his hand and flicked it on. She leaned back so he had to come further inside the doorway. He stuck his arm in holding the light out to her. She hurled her body at the door as hard as she could. She caught Nicky Grasso's head and arm in the crack. He shrieked and tried to pull out of the trap. She pushed harder, rammed again and again at the door. Nicky's face turned pale and sweat dropped off it. Suddenly his eyes rolled up in his head and he sagged to the floor.

She stepped over him and rushed out into the main part of the house. In the living room she glanced this way and that to find the door outside. She had seen dogs out there, but she didn't care right now. She simply had to get out.

Then she remembered the gun she had seen drop to the floor beside Nicky Grasso's body. She ran back to the hallway and picked it up. Breathing heavily, she turned to go back to the living room, but Nicky's powerful hand snaked out and grabbed her ankle.

141

She screamed. Nicky pulled her down to the floor. She scrambled along the carpeting, clawing it with her fingernails. Nicky's powerful hand pulled her toward him. He was growling with anger now, his lips almost frothing. She tried to pull away, but he was holding her by the wrist now, thrusting himself onto her. Her trousers were unzipped, her jacket pinned back to reveal her tight blouse. She panted, she gasped, she tried to kick him in the groing.

He slowly spreadeagled her on the carpet. His face was close to hers, blowing the stink of his breath into her eyes and hair. She writhed and arched her back and he laughed and swore at her, words that were Italian and not understood by her, words that were obscenities that did not matter anyway.

She felt control of her body leaving her in the painful assault on her flesh and she stopped struggling.

He threw her into the room, dumped her on the bed, and locked the door when he was done. She heard him light another roach and blow it through the cracks of the door.

She felt sick.

"Hey spik," said Nicky through the door.

"Screw," she said.

"You pretty good for a gook."

He giggled and blew pot.

There was a big map pinned to the wall of the study. It showed the entire United States. There were hundreds of pins set into the map, some in the states, and some in the ocean near the borders.

Tom Galey stood in front of the map and waved at it. In a chair, Major Fong looked up at him.

"We've got a bomb in every one of those specified areas, Major. And each area is a small or large refinery, producing field, storage area, or drilling rig. We've even got bombs planted on the offshore rigs. They're attached to the pump lines out of sight."

"How can you be sure they won't be removed before you activate them?" Major Fong asked.

"A good question," smiled Galey. "In some instances, the bombs are *inside* the storage tanks. That means they *can't* be discovered. They're limpet mines; they stick to the sides where they will wait until activated. As for those on the outer surfaces of the refinery pipes and tanks, we think they won't be found. Besides, in some cases those refineries are connected to others nearby through pipe lines. This chemical mix will burn along the pipe lines like a fuse burns, until the fire reaches the next in line."

Major Fong scratched his stomach. "Hau!" he said. "That's good."

"We think it's foolproof," said Galey, allowing himself the indulgence of a faint smile.

"I.shall message the General tonight."

"Good. We're all ready to go, you understand?"

"I understand. Now, if you'll give me those figures again?"

Galey nodded. "Okay. We figure the total U.S. reserves at this point to be at least fifty-five billion, six hundred million barrels. And we've got bombs that will ignite every one of them. As for the drilling operations, we figure the biggies alone for one million fifty thousand a day from Exxon, one hundred and twenty thousand a day from Shell, eight hundred and fifty thousand a day from Texaco, four hundred thousand a day from Mobil, six hundred thousand a day from Standard Oil of California, and four hundred thousand a day from Gulf.

"The independents have some more, of course. I won't even bother to estimate that. With all this

143

gone up in flames, Major, you can see that the oil industry in the United States will be in chaos. Even if all the fires are put out in a week—which would be an absolutely stunning accomplishment in its magnitude, it would take months for the industry to get back on its feet. The United States consumes seventeen million barrels of oil a day. That means that the OPEC with total reserves of at least three hundred and sixty-seven billion barrels from the Middle East alone, would be able to raise its prices as high as it wanted to serve the U.S. With the United States, Japan, and Europe all clamoring for oil, their economies would be completely thrown out of control and we, with the help of the Soviet Union and the Arab States, could control the economy of the world."

Major Fong smiled. "Of course, you are simply pointing out the obvious. That is the reason for Operation Lamp, anyway. Interesting, title, no? Lamp? Oil for the lamp, you see?"

Galey stared stonily.

"Captain," said Major Fond slowly. "You have told me how the bombs are built, how they operate, and how they have been attached to some part of every refinery, producing field, storage area, and drill on the map." He gestured to the wall. "But you haven't told me how the bombs will be detonated."

Galey nodded. He reached over to the table beside which the Major was seated. "Cigarette?" he asked, extending his packet of Camels to the Major.

Major Fong blinked as if annoyed at being drawn from the subject of his question. Then he reached out and took one.

"Thank you."

Galey reached for the lighter on the table near the pile of papers and maps. He flicked it and a flame shot from the top of the small oil well mounted on

144

the lighter.

The Major leaned into the flame and got his cigarette going. He moved back and watched Galey through his almond shaped eyes. "Well?"

Galey blew smoke through his nostrils and tossed the small oil well lighter up into the air. "Neat gadgets, aren't they? These little plastic oil wells? Petroleum Institute sent them out to everybody. All the oil companies. It's the biggest association of oil producing companies in the country."

"I'm sure it is," snapped the Major in open annoyance. "But I was asking you a question, Captain!"

Galey studied the small lighter in his hand and set it down on the table within reach.

"When you flick the wheel, flames shoot from the top of the oil well, Major." He smiled. "It's that simple."

"What's that simple?"

"Activating the incendiaries."

There was a long silence. "I fail to comprehend, Captain Galey!"

Galey picked up the lighter again and turned it over. He put his fingernail into a screw in the bottom, and turned it. He pulled out the plug showed the Major. "You fill it up with fluid here, Major."

Major Fong was not amused. He said so.

Galey tightened the screw once again, and put his thumb into another screw beside that one. "You pull this one out and you can see that it's not really a part of the lighter at all." He showed the Major.

The Major's eyes narrowed as he studied the small cylinder in Galey's hand and there was a flicker of understanding in his eyes.

"Yes. It's a solid-state transistor receiver-transmitter, capable of broadcasting a signal to a distance of twenty miles. The radio is capable of receiving a signal from a distance of three thousand miles. A nice little job. Japanese made, really."

The Major licked his lips.

Galey laughed. "That's right. We simply send a master signal to these little beauties, which are located all over the country where there are producing oil wells, where there are storage fields, where there are refineries, and—pow! The little oil well lighters receive and transmit the signal to the bombs." Galley set down the lighter. "Dante's Inferno would be heaven compared to the United States of America with all that oil on fire."

CHAPTER TEN

Captain of Detectives William O. Dekker was furious. He ground his teeth as he watched the half dozen underlings going about their business in the small but cluttered apartment of Moon Chu Ling-doo.

To lower his blood pressure, Dekker paced back and forth like a show off lion at feeding time—left, right, left, right—with one fist smacking into the other palm as he raged inwardly.

He was too saturated in his own venom to realize that he was being observed with both trepidation and amusement by Danny Bolton of P.I Security. Bolton was there out of sheer blind chance. He had come back to Dekker's office in the morning to discuss the disappearance of the Kung Fu Phantom from the Legion Temple the night before. The two of them had just started to chew over Victor Mace when the call came in about the mess at the Chinese gash's digs.

Putting two and two together—the fact that Mace was Chinese and the fact that the owner of the massacre apartment was a chinko broad—Dekker had grabbed his hat and coat and headed out to the site of the blooding with Bolton in tow.

"I put two and two together and I get Victor Mace," he said sharply. "What about you?"

Bolton nodded. "It's got to be. There's some tie-up with this Chinese girl."

"How do you know that?" Dekker grumbled.

"I *don't* know. It's just logical."

Dekker slapped his palm with his fist. "I'm going to send off a rocket to Washington. I want that damned C.I.A. bunch closed down. That miserable chink is driving me up the wall."

"It's not that easy to get around the C.I.A.," Bolton warned.

"No?" Dekker stared. Then he suddenly cooled down. "Yeah. You're right, Danny." He slumped visibly. With that he pulled Bolton over with him and they sank into the couch together. The crime lab photographer was shooting stills of the bedroom and Dekker could see the flashes out of the corner of his eye as he leaned closer to Bolton. "How do we get rid of those two? The Chinaman and the Mexican?"

Bolton's face was expressionless. "Maybe I can work out something."

"Maybe you better." Dekker's voice was very low. "Look. I've got fifteen D.O.A.s from the night before last. I've got two corpses and a possible three from the Legion Temple riot. And I've got three more after last night. This goddamned chink is puttng me out of business! Sure, the corpses so far are only hit men and no-known-addresses of one kind or another. But wait till some innocent John gets whiffed. Then I got the Commissioner and the Oil Muguls *and* the Space Agency heads—I've got them all on my back whipping me to cut down the crime wave!"

Bolton's eyes narrowed. "I think the chink's hiding out at the pod."

"Christ, I can't hit the pod. I'm not supposed to know it exists! What's worse, on the bottom line, I'm supposed to *cooperate* with the bastards! How the hell can I move against the pod and get the Kung Fu creep?"

"You want me to con him again?"

Dekker stared witheringly at Bolton. "You did one hell of a half-assed job for me the last night, now didn't you, Danny-boy?"

Bolton flushed. He looked angry enough to punch Dekker, but then he wrestled to get himself in control and spoke like sandpaper rubbing against concrete:

"The Chinese girl wasn't in the scenario. Sure, I blew it. But I didn't know about the yellow bird."

"Who the hell were those damned goons anyway?" Dekker muttered, his mind trying to come to grips with that knotty problem once again. "We had that thing set up perfectly. But then out of thin air we get some crazy fools shooting up a riot in one corner of the auditorium, and then we get a half-dozen flying hatchet men out of the blue trying to chop our pigeon."

Bolton's face hardened. "I'll accept the blame for the fact we lost Mace," he said. "But don't think I can clue you in to everything."

Dekker sagged back against the couch, suddenly exhausted. "I don't blame you for anything, Danny. I just want results."

"I want to help," Bolton said, staring at the carpet where fresh blood had clotted in a large round pattern within the past several hours.

"Then help," grated Dekker.

"Okay. Here's what I'm going to do. Frank Wainwright is a tough old boy. He's my boss, head of the Petroleum Institute. He's in with the Oil

Boys; he's one of them. Now I go to him and I tell him what's been bugging me. I mean, about the corpses and the trouble. He asks me how I know about it. I tell him I'm working with the pod on this thing, under orders from the Hub."

Dekker looked sulky. "They'll have your ass, boy."

"No way. Wainwright knows his share of movers in Washington. Hell, the Oil Boys own half of Congress. He can get through on a conduit to the Hub. We get the Director of C.I.A. to call off the pod. *Then* we get the Kung Fu kid out of our hair for good."

"I don't like too many people getting into the act," sighed Dekker.

"Give me forty-eight hours."

"You've had forty-eight hours! You promised me you'd give me the pigtail two days ago! All I've got is two dozen salamis on marble slabs!"

Bolton bit his lip. "Give me time, Captain!"

"What else have I got?" Dekker muttered.

"You've got a good lead here," Bolton said, inspired by Dekker's glum countenance.

"You crapping me?"

"No! The Chinese girl! Find out how she fits in. Who does she work for?"

Dekker came to life slightly. "Don't tell me how to do my job, sonny boy! I've already got the lines out on that. Turns out she works for Public Broadcasting System at KHOU-TV. How about that?" He almost smiled. "Anyway, I'm going to question her boss myself."

"See? This is a real break, instead of the end of the world!"

"Don't try to silvertongue me, Danny. I've had enough of your double talk for a lifetime!" He glared viciously at Bolton. "You've got forty-eight hours!

That's it!" He began roaring. "Now get off your ass and start pulling wires!"

"And *you* give me that tape on McCready!" retorted Bolton.

"It's on ice," Dekker said through narrowed eyes. "Don't worry. Nobody'll connect you with Big Red." There was a pause. "Except me. And I won't use it —unless you fail to hand me that chinko pretty goddamned quick!"

Danny Bolton went down in the elevator alone. He was scared shitless. Everything was coming apart. Dekker was teed off totally, and would shake all the apples out the tree if he didn't get Victor Mace delivered to him on a platter, ready for the barbecue sauce.

And how the hell could Bolton produce the Chinese menace? What a shambles. It had all been so tight and controlled. And the money McCready had paid him was beautiful—long and green and lovely. It was in the bank, every penny of it. Five yards to give McCready access to the warehouse where the Petroleum Institute kept old records and tax data.

"What you want in the warehouse?" Bolton asked McCready—the late Big Red McCready, that is, Bolton recalled sorrowfully as he thought back now.

"Nothing in the warehouse, Danny. I've got a client wants to *use* the premises."

"What for?"

McCready was amused. "For a security ace, you're a pretty stupid gee. Don't you ever look at a map?"

"What map?" muttered Bolton, feeling like a horse's ass.

"The goddamned warehouse back up to a branch of the Houston Citizens Bank. Don't you even know where the warehouse is?"

"Sure! It's out near the NASA Johnson Space

151

Center by Clear Lake City. What the hell's that got to do—?",

"I'll trade five yards for the keys to the shed."

Bolton blinked. "Five grand?"

"You heard right."

"You mean they're going to drill through the back of the goddamned warehouse into the bank vault?"

"I don't worry about what they're going to do, Danny. I just get them what they ask for, you know? And what they're asking for is access to the Petroleum Institute warehouse near Clear Lake City."

"Well—"

"Also. I've got to know the security regulations involving the night guard."

"Sure. I've got that in the book. No sweat."

"Get me the key, Danny-boy, and I'll have it back to you within two hours."

"But—"

"They'll make it look like they forced their way in! You won't be on the hook. Those guys are pros!"

"Who are they?" Bolton was beginning to sweat.

"Never mind who they are. They're friends of mine." McCready grinned. "I always been a friend of yours, right, Danny? That makes them friends of yours, too."

"With friends like that, I could be making mattresses in the state pen."

"Okay," said McCready. "So once in a while I run around with guys with long rap sheets. Is it a crime? These guys are just out to turn a buck or two. It's an easy gig. Drill through, take the money, and run. For five gees, why should you complain?"

Bolton grunted. Inflation was eating up everything he had. He had been prepared to retire once at fifty-five, but the damned ex-wife who had got her claws into everything he had ruined that scheme. With the five grand he could get something started now.

152

Maybe McCready would come up with more scams in the future. Maybe this was just one egg of many that could be laid by the goose in McCready's pocket.

"Lay the five on me," said Bolton with a sigh.

"Two-five now, and two-five after the heist."

"You're on."

And it was as simple as that. There had been no flak at all about the heist. In fact, Bolton had never even seen the bank job mentioned in the paper. There were probably so many safes cracked in the course of a week in Texas that there wouldn't be enough type left to set up the stories if they ran each one.

And no one had said a word about the break-in at the warehouse. In fact Bolton had visited the site himself. There wasn't even a sign of the entry into the bank building through the wall. They had apparently nailed the wall back together to cover their tracks.

Bolton banked the two-five up front, and later the two-five on completion. There was no quarrel about the cash. McCready was pleased, Bolton was pleased.

And he forgot all about it.

Until the night when McCready died.

Jesus! It was like the lightning had struck and the sky had fallen. Big Red McCready—a guard on the offshore rig where fifteen corpses had bloomed like evil flowers in the night! Jesus H. Christ . . .

Of course Bolton never let anybody know about his tie-in with McCready. Shatford knew nothing about it. Shat was Bolton's right hand, and even he hadn't tumbled to the Houston Citizens Bank caper. Nor had he tumbled to the fact that Bolton knew McCready. Bolton cleverly had brought up the subject of McCready and Dekker with Shatford, pretending he was seeking some way to get information about the oil rig massacre. Selling out the chink had pulled the wool over Shat's eyes, sure as God mad little green apples.

Yeah.

And then the pitch to Dekker, which was the nut of the deal. He make it look like a reasonable trade to Dekker. What he wanted, he got. He had to play it tight to the chest. He said he had crossed paths with McCready in the past. He said he was afraid the P.I. biggies would find out. He said with the investigation of McCready's death, he might be mentioned as McCready's partner in a venture many years ago.

It was true, of course, because he and McCready had known each other in their home town in the Staked Plains, West Texas. Ropesville, out near Lubbock. Would you believe it? That was the place where their paths had crossed.

It would look bad, Bolton told Dekker.

Dekker saw the light. Dekker wanted Mace. Bolton offered up Mace on a straight trade. Beautiful. Because now Bolton knew Dekker hadn't got anything out of McCready before McCready died. The deal to hand over Mace had worked like a charm, right up to the last split second. Bolton had conned the Chinese into meeting him at Legion Temple. And then Bolton had put the icing on the cake by hiring six goons to button up the chink in case he managed to slip out of the trap they'd set.

But it had all caved in at the last minute. Jesus. There was Mace caught tight as a Scotsman. And there was Dekker, drooling at the mouth to get the chink in the slammer. The son of a bitch went up like Puff the Magic Dragon! Even Bolton's backup punks had been zapped by the Kung Fu creep.

Who was the Chinese girl, anyway? And who were

154

the boobs who had tied to waste Mace in her apartment?

Those weren't the only questions Bolton wanted answered. Who had killed McCready? How had he got into that oil rig deal? Who was he working for that time? Jesus, Bolton knew a set-up when he saw it. And McCready had set up the offshore rig.

For the Chinese Reds?

Bolton almost popped his cookies when he thought about the Reds. How the hell had Mc-Cready crossed over to that bunch? Or was it simply a job?

Tough shit.

McCready was dead. They'd killed him after the big one.

And Bolton had worked himself off the butcher's hook. He left the apartment building and climbed into his big Mercury with the air conditioning, the four-track stereo, the portable bar in the back seat, and the mink-lined seats and smiled as he drove out of the parking lot and headed back for the loop.

It was as he approached the graceful overpass of Interstate 45 which formed the western boundary of the Houston loop that his associational chambers suddenly posed him an interesting question.

If McCready had worked for the Red Chinese on the offshore rig, could he possibly have been working for the Red Chinese when he entered the Petroleum Institute's warehouse? Was the bank job a screen? Was there something in the warehouse they were after?

Was it Mao Tse-tung who had wanted in? What could've been inside that warehouse that the Reds wanted, enough to pay five yards for?

The air conditioning purred and blew soft air over Bolton's sweat-covered forehead. What in hell could have been in that warehouse that they wanted?

CHAPTER ELEVEN

The wool-wrapped oars made only the most muffled of sounds as the rowboat moved through the darkened waters of the lake.

Mace felt a finger tap his right shoulder. He turned. Juarez put his mouth close to Mace's ear.

"There it is." He pointed.

Mace could not even see Juarez's hand, it was that dark. He peered ahead in the night and saw the lake shore rising vaguely from the water level of Lake Houston. They had launched the rowboat back at Alexander Deussen Park, and rowed quietly along the perimeter of the wooded area until they had come to the shoreline drive of Lake Houston Parkway that bordered Dwight D. Eisenhower Park. Now they were moving along the large estates that fronted the lake. Not three feet from the shore the cyclone fence lifted into the air—twelve feet high, just as the specs had said.

Mace nodded. His eyes were searching out the outline of the ranch house beyond the rise, with the lights which should be in the windows, but he could not make it out.

Juarez shrugged and went on steering.

Now, in Lake Houston, the rowboat suddenly touched ground.

Mace raised a hand. Quietly they shipped oars and then Mace pushed one oar down and touched the rocky slope of the lake bottom as it became shoreline. Sculling with the oar's tip, he drove the rowboat up onto the pebbly beach and jumped out. The splash he made was almost unheard in the night. Somewhere crickets were booming away and a dog howled.

Juarez was right behind him, standing on the shore, dragging the prow of the boat up onto the pebbly shore.

Quickly Mace laid the oars in the boat's bottom and gave another tug to bring it up safely out of the water so it would not drift away. Then he turned to Juarez and tapped him on the shoulder. Juarez nodded. He gathered up the black bag he had brought and slung it over his shoulder. Mace touched his many-pocketed coveralls dyed black for night cover and adjusted the hood that hid all of his head except for his eyes, nose and mouth.

He pointed along the fence.

Juarez followed as Mace picked his way carefully over the rocks and clefts in the eroded shore line that dropped down from the edge of the electrified fence surrounding the Lazy G Rancho.

According to the scouting reports given to Juarez, the best place to attack the electrified fence was on the southern quadrant about halfway from the highway to the lake. There a ravine cut through the straight fence, meandering toward the lake with its occasional flash flood overflow of quick storm run-off.

In minutes they found the ravine just where Juarez's map man had showed it to be and picked their way up the rock-strewn gulch toward the fence. And there it was, rising quickly into the air and topped by a triple-strand of barbed wire which crossed each fence support over glistening white insulators.

Mace signaled Juarez to stand by while he crawled forward in the dusty ravine and got to within six inches of the fence. His eye traveled up along the strands of the innocent-looking square-woven metal knit and saw the small plastic discs that held the horizontal wires away from the verticals. The three wires at the top were electrified; so were four more woven cleverly into the regular mesh.

Mace held his hand out toward Juarez, and instantly the C.I.A. case officer laid a long strand of insulated wire in Mace's. Then came a pair of rubber-insulated electrician's pliers. Mace quickly went to work scraping the insulation off the end of the wire and hooked the bare end onto the bottom hot wire at a point on the right-hand slope of the drainage gulch. He crimped it in place, and then moved over to the left-hand side of the gulch and attached the other end of the wire to the same hot wire about three feet from the other. The six feet of added tap wire now hung down into the ravine.

Quickly Juarez gave him three more, and Mace attached them to the other hot wires so that all the hot wires were bypassed with the four parallels. Mace put his finger to his lips and moved forward, poising the open pliers at the middle of the lowest hot wire. Quickly Mace clamped down on the handles and the hot wire snapped in two. A tiny spark flicked against the pliers, but that was all.

Quietly they waited for the hue and cry. No. The bypass had carried the current. Whatever change there had been in the amperage flow had not registered on the alarm system in Galey's house.

Now Mace snipped the second, third, and fourth hot wires. He had told Juarez before exactly what he was doing so that Juarez would be ready to help him if need be.

Now Mace went to work on the cold wires, snipping them quickly from bottom up. Then he handed the pliers back to Juarez and began pulling back the edges of the fence where he had nipped the wires to form an opening large enough for a human body.

Mace waved at Juarez. Juarez nodded and came forward. A rock slid down the slope of the small dry gulch.

Both Mace and Juarez froze. Mace saw the shadowy form first. It loomed above them outside the fence, on the top of the slope to the gulley. There was a rifle or shotgun in the grip of the man's hand. He held it with the barrel pointing down at Mace and Juarez.

"Freeze or I'll shoot," a Texas drawl warned them.

Mace was already moving. Quickly he rose to his full height, turned to the right, away from the fence, and made one jump halfway up the slope. As he landed on his right foot he sprang back to the left, continuing up the slope, but now headed directly at the shadowy figure who had the rifle.

Before the guard could even move the gun to center it on either Mace or Juarez, Mace's hand had gripped the tip of the barrel and flipped it aside. The man gave a surprised cry, like a cat mewing, and Mace slammed into his lower legs, grabbing the ankles. Immediately he upended the startled guard, flipping him over on his back.

"Ugh," the man said. Mace crouched over him, giving him a *Hiraken* closed knuckle punch to the solar plexus. The man's abdominal muscles ruptured at the force of the blow, and he sank back in paralysis. Mace quickly lifted the rifle from the

160

ground and removed the rounds.

A small walkie-talkie rolled out from the pocket of the guard's windbreaker. Mace turned to Juarez, and Juarez quickly scooped it up, holding it to his ear.

"That you, Judd?" a voice asked on the mini-radio.

Juarez wrinkled up his nose and closed his eyes. "Nothing to worry about," he said, in a close approximation of the unconscious guard's voice. "Turned my damned ankle. I'm okay."

"Ugh," grunted the other guard and the walkie-talkie switched off.

Mace shook his head. He pointed to himself, and then pointed down along the fence. His meaning was obvious. Juarez nodded. Mace then indicated the fence, and pointed to Juarez to stay there. Mace picked up the emptied-out rifle and the walkie-talkie and started out boldly along the fence. He could see the other man not twenty yards from him as he came up the hill. Now he could see the house, too, with lights on in three of the windows on the ground floor. It was a rambling structure, surrounded by a lush garden and trees.

Five yards from the other man, the guard approaching him stopped. "What the hell, Judd? You don't—"

Mace dropped the rifle which encumbered him and sprinted toward the guard. The guard was raising his rifle just as Mace leaped up in the air and clipped him in the neck with a left-footed sword-foot kick. The guard's neck artery was smashed and he plunged over into oblivion.

Mace emptied the rifle and ran back to Juarez.

"In," he whispered. "Come on! Have you got the hypos?"

Juarez had the hypos out of the black bag and

161

handed them to Mace. "Good."

They scrambled through the cut part of the fence and went up the short slope to the main back yard of the big estate. Mace signaled to Juarez to run, pointing to the house which was now outlined in the darkness. As they came up the rise Mace could see the forms of four huge dogs fanning out and beginning to circle in on them. Two were growling low in their throats. Dobermans. Mace waved Juarez back. Juarez halted. Mace paused where he was. There were four Dobermans, and that was all. Mace saw the first one begin to come in toward his right. The second one turned and approached from the left. They had been trained well. The third and fourth dogs simply stood in back, waiting. They would have their role to play once the first two performed theirs.

The first Doberman leaped through the air, going for Mace's throat. Mace could see the white teeth in the darkness as the upper lip curled back. The mouth opened silently, and the big dog sailed for Mace's throat as straight as an arrow.

Mace went down on his back, thrusting up with both feet just as the Doberman landed on him. Instantly Mace reached out his right hand and stabbed the dog's front leg with the hypodermic needle Juarez had given him. It was a typical plastic one-time-use hypodermic hospital needle, filled with an animal tranquilizer supplied by the C.I.A.'s Technical Services Division.

The Doberman rolled on over Mace's body and crashed to the ground behind him, lying there inert. The tranquilizer worked in split seconds, the T.S.D. wizards had said. True. The second Doberman was a pushover. Mace had gained his feet by the time the second leaped him. The needle went in through the chest, just beside the breast bone. Now number three and number four were circling warily, closing in on Mace from the flanks. Mace was in a pincers. Dog three was moving in from the left, and dog four from the right. He could take care of them one at a time, except that he could not get at one before the other. They were timing their attack on him simultaneously.

Mace whirled, throwing one needle like a small pub dart at the right hand dog. Then, quickly, he wheeled around, 180 degrees, and faced the dog on the left. The big black Doberman was on him, snarling and gnashing his teeth, slobbering all over Mace with the stinking saliva from his throat.

The Kung Fu Master slipped the needle onto the dog's side and the dog rolled off him, instantly asleep.

"Mace!" hissed Juarez.

But the cry came too late.

The third Doberman had not been pierced by the hypodermic needle Mace had hurled at him. He had dodged it and was now pummeling Mace to the ground.

The sharp teeth sank into Mace's shoulder, tearing and ripping away at the flesh. Mace knew that the dog's teeth would cling to him until either he or the dog died. The Doberman had been trained that way. Mace was mortified that his tranquilizer had failed to stop the dog.

Instantly, raising his left hand in a *Shuto* knife-edge chop, he slammed the blade of his hand bone into the dog's neck, breaking the backbone and sending the dog immediately into paralysis and death.

The dog whimpered as he released his teeth from Mace's shoulder muscles and sank to the ground.

Angry at himself, Mace ran back to Juarez, holding his shoulder with his left hand. "Bandage me up,

Benny," he whispered. "I've goofed badly."

Juarez was instantly at work, tearing up sulfa packs and inundating the bleeding area with antiseptic. Then he wrapped a pad quickly over the wound and tied it with bandage.

"Come on," Mace said finally. "We've got to get know we're here!"

They ran toward the house, through the garden that was laid out in back of it. Mace had studied the layout on the blueprints for many hours and knew exactly what to do.

The blueprints did not show the black man who worked for Galey as a gardener. He was mentally incompetent. He did not really know what he was doing. An ex-boxer who had been brain-scrambled a dozen times, he liked to walk about the estate in the dead of night.

He saw Mace before Mace saw him.

He reared up and struck with a heavy Karate chop and Mace went down without knowing what had hit him. The big man turned to Juarez, and leaped at him, swinging his huge hambone fists at his head. He had already killed one man, in a ring encounter. Juarez would be number two.

Moon Chu Lingdoo opened the bureau drawer with absolute silence. It wouldn't do to let that Neanderthal bully in the hallway hear her. He would look in to see what she was up to. And until she wanted him to know, she would cover her moves.

Bruised and battered, her anger deeply banked but smouldering within her, she had rested the balance of the day until she had heard her boss and the Chinese menace come back from wherever they had gone. Now they were in the study. She could hear the low murmur of their voices through the wall. But

164

she was unable to understand a word.

She knew now she should have tried to get away after Nicky Grasso had left her in her room, but she had been too stunned.

The folder of matches was in the upper drawer with the cigarettes. She had found them there when she had first come into the room. Her dialogue with Nicky asking for a smoke had been bluff. Now she drew the matches out and took the newspaper she had carefully wadded up page by page under the covers of the bed so no one would hear her and placed it in the wastebasket next to the door.

Holding the paper and match under the cover of the bedclothes, she struck the match and got a flame going. Then she took the flaming newspaper out from under the blanket and touched it to the pile of paper in the basket. Instantly flames shot upward, halfway to the ceiling.

"Fire!" she said, her face close to the door. She wanted Nicky to hear, but not Mr. Galey and the Chinese bastard. "My God! The room's on fire."

There was instant reaction from outside the door. She could hear Nicky leaning against the panels, probably sniffing the air for smoke. He smelled it. Moon was waving the gray fumes toward the crack.

"You damned little fool!" muttered Nicky, and quickly unlocked the door.

Moon was holding a four-legged chair above her head and when the door opened inwardly and Nicky's head appeared, she smashed it down with all her might. The front leg of the chair struck Nicky's left temple and blood instantly appeared. The head sagged, with Nicky's shoulder slamming against the door and pushing it open farther. The gun clanked on the floor under him, and luckily did not fire.

Moon stepped swiftly over the crumpled body of

the hit man. Without a moment's pause, she ran down the corridor toward the rear of the house where she had entered the back door with Mr. Galey the night before.

She could see the kitchen door ahead of her. The room she was passing was the study where Mr. Galey had sat with her.

"No!" she heard Galey shout in anger. "I'll be damned if I'm going to wait for orders from Peking! I'm in charge of this operation, and *I* say when it goes up!"

"Absolutely not!" snapped the Major in instant reaction. "I will not allow it! We must have confirmation from the General! The time the storage dumps blow up must be integrated with the time the People's Republic acts! There must be absolute synchronization!"

"The hell with synchronization! Those bombs are ready to go, and I say when they're ready they go. Your goddamned general and your bureaucrats can kiss my ass if they want to. They'd better synchronize themselves with the minute the tanks go up."

"I could kill you right now, Captain Galey," raged Major Fong. "I would not jeopardize the mission one bit! Someone else—"

"Who knows how to blow those devices?" jeered Galey. "No one but me!"

Moon was arrested in her flight. What devices? What explosion? What was all this talk of synchronization?

"I know about the oil well lighters, Captain Galey," Major Fong retorted tauntingly. "I know how the detonators are placed in them. I know that much—and that's enough to find out the rest."

"Bullshit," shouted Galey. "I'm on the hook with this operation. The authorities aren't dumb. They're onto me. I know it. I'm really on the rock pile. Cap-

166

tain Dekker tried to contact me this afternoon. If he'd known where we were, he'd have nailed me. Look. I've got only a couple more hours freedom before the whole thing blows. I've *got* to press the button."

There was a moment's silence. "You press the button, or whatever it is you press to turn that fifty-five billion barrels of oil into fire and I'll guarantee you one thing, Captain Galey. I'll guarantee you that I'll kill you within minutes."

"Your threats resemble the clanging of cracked bells," snapped Galey.

"The Chairman's words?" mocked Major Fong.

"The Captain's words," said Galey.

"I'll get on the shortwave to my cut-out," said Major Fong, abruptly backing down. "But I want it clearly understood you're not to blow those tanks until I get the word from the General."

"It'll be too late," cried Galey. "I'm on the hot seat! I've got to move, or I'll never be able to."

"You'll move when I say so, and you'll make those bombs work, or you're a dead man."

Moon was frozen in her tracks. Bombs? Fifty-five billion barrels of oil? What was that all about? She had come into the Chinese People's Social Affairs Department because she believed in the truth of communism. It was a way of sharing the good things of the earth. It was a way of doing away with violence and the savagery of war. Sure, it took a little twisting of an arm and a leg here and there, but in the end it would mean peace and quiet and the world at rest.

What the hell was all this about blowing up the oil supplies of America? What in the hell was this about setting the country on fire? Moon's heart sank. She knew, quite suddenly and quite completely, that she had been sold a bill of goods. She had been conned, jived, really worked over and used. Yes, goddamn it, used! Not only her body, but her mind and her psyche.

The dirty little shits! People's world? Social revolution? A beautiful place to live? A likely story. She was part of some kind of really evil conspiracy. And Mr. Galey was in it, too. Always the smooth-talker. Always the dedicated media man. Always the balanced programming advocate. Fooey. A goddamned anti-American, that's what he really was! Well, so was she—to a certain extent. She didn't like bombing the Vietnamese and going to war over oil, but she'd be damned if she wanted to blow up the energy supply of the country!

If that was what they were talking about. And it certainly seemed that they were. What were these oil well lighters? Then she remembered. She had seen one in Galey's study. So *that*—

"Listen here, you Maoist slob," Galey was growling, "I'll detonate those bombs the first thing in the morning. Then we're free and clear of the law. Otherwise I'm a dead duck. And you can tell the General and the Chairman and the goddamned Dalai Lama if you want that it's going to be that way!"

There was a sudden motion and the door beside which Moon was standing was wrenched open. Galey came bursting through it, stopping in shock when he saw Moon there.

"What the hell—?"

"What is it?" Major Fong asked over Galey's shoulder.

Galey grabbed Moon by the shoulder as she wheeled and tried to run. "I don't know, but I think it's our little China mug with the too big ears." Major Fong pushed past Galey and the two men stared at Moon as she cringed in Galey's grip.

"Kill her," snapped Major Fong, his eyes narrowing.

"I won't do anything!" Moon screamed. "Let me go!"

Galey shook her till her teeth rattled. "Quiet down. You bet your sweet little ass you won't do anything!"

"Kill her," repeated Major Fong.

"Shut up!" yelled Galey. "You touch her and I'll put a bullet between your slanty little eyes!"

Major Fong was suddenly stiff and silent. He gazed at Galey with hatred and frustrated savagery. He said nothing.

"You heard us, didn't you?" Galey asked, shaking her. She blinked her eyes, trying to smile at him. She could always smile and get what she wanted from him. But now it didn't work. He shook her harder.

"What did you hear?"

"No-o-othing," she gasped out.

"You heard!" said Galey. He stared at her, his face twisted now, his eyes darting from one side to the other. She thought he suddenly looked quite sinister, like an unmasked demon of some kind. She was frightened.

"She knows about the oil well lighters?" Major Fong asked in a quiet voice. "And she knows about the incendiary bombs? And she knows about the fifty-five billion barrels of oil going up in smoke?" He chuckled abruptly, his laughter bubbling up like crude oil in the processing pipes.

"We'll have to kill her," said Galey in an unemotional voice. He stared at her, his lips tight against his teeth. "Tough shit, baby. Sorry your ears are bigger than your brains."

"Let her go, Mr. Galey," a strangely trembling voice said from the darkness of the corridor behind her. It was Nicky Grasso.

Galey swung around, gripping Moon until tears came to her eyes.

169

The Major rushed forward as his right foot came down, he was bending forward, and slashing out at Nicky Grasso's head with his right hand bunched into what Moon thought looked exactly like a club. It was more Kung Fu stuff! The Major was apparently an expert.

Moon ran. She used the excitement of the moment to flee down the hallway toward the kitchen and the back door of the ranch house. Galey was still watching the Major as he worked over Nicky Grasso. So shocked was he that he did not even notice Moon had left.

She banged through the back door and rushed out into the night, trying to make out the shadowy shapes of the garden. She knew the whole estate was electrified, but she was only thinking about a temporary haven from Galey and the Chinese Major. Galey was shouting after her, his feet banging on the kitchen floor.

Moon ran harder. Suddenly, in front of her, two figures seemed to loom in the darkness. One, by the shape of him, she recognized as the demented black gardner who was a stumblebum reject from the ring. He was swinging his hands at a second man. Now Moon could see a third lying on the ground.

The big man heard her and turned.

At that instant the man whom he had been attacking struck out and felled the giant by a solid blow to the genitals.

Juarez grabbed the girl. "Get me out of here!" sobbed the girl. "Get me out of here." She didn't care who it was or why the two men were there. She only knew that she had found an ally.

The door opened in the house and a man stood silhouetted there. Galey. He was looking out and shouting:

"Pete, you black bastard! Stop the girl!"

170

Juarez held onto Moon, tugged at the man on the ground, who stirred, and the three of them began stumbling through the darkness. The night erupted with shots fired from the house. The Major's voice thundered in the darkness: "Kill her, Captain Galey!"

CHAPTER TWELVE

In a motel out on Interstate 45 near Halls Bayou
Mace and Juarez sat with a weeping and almost
hysterical Moon Chu Lingdoo.

They had fled the Lazy G Rancho through the
same hole Mace had cut in the electrified fence, had
retraced their steps to the rowboat, and had rowed
back across the lake to Juarez's minibus.

No one had pursued. They could hear in the distance the cries of the house personnel apparently
trying to put out the fire Moon had started in her
prison room.

"I didn't know he meant to have you killed!" she
shrieked at Mace in the car, when she had realized
finally that she had been rescued by the man she
had enticed to her apartment and set up for murder.

Mace shrugged that off. Both he and Juarez were
more concerned about the reason for Moon's break
with Galey and Major Fong.

Once they got in the motel, they brought her slowly
back to consciousness, sent out for coffee and sand-
wiches, and began the tedious process of interrogation.

"My boss told me that you were working with the C.I.A.," she sobbed. "He told me the C.I.A. was trying to ruin our liberal programming at KHOU-TV. That's why I followed Victor Mace and got him to my apartment. It was just a kind of trick to pound some sense into him."

It sounded logical, anyway, Mace admitted to himself. The girl might well be simply a misguided zealot who had signed on with the Mao Reds without knowing what they were up to.

"Who were the men?"

"I don't know," she wailed. "When I ran out, I found my boss there. I didn't even see the men."

"So Galey set it up," Mace muttered.

"Yes," said Moon.

"And where did you go?" Juarez asked.

"He made me sit down in his Caddy. It was parked in the back lot of the apartment building."

"And then?"

"Pretty soon he came down and we drove off to his place. I asked him what had happened. He told me Mr. Mace had been roughed up, just as a warning, and that the apartment was a mess. He'd have to take me home with him. There would be police and questions."

Juarez and Mace eyed one another.

"Okay. Then what happened?"

Moon bit her lip. "I began to see a little more clearly that I'd been put on. There was this grisly intelligence Major."

"Major Fong."

"How'd you know?"

"Never mind."

"He was just awful. And I got a different impression in the house. Although my boss tried to cover it over, the Major kept talking about getting rid of Victor Mace. When he was told that you had escaped, the Major went into a fit.

"Then when I was running out I heard the Major and Mr. Galey in a terrible fight. They were shouting at the top of their lungs. I couldn't help but overhear what they were talking about. They were discussing setting oil supplies on fire all across the United States."

Mace looked up. "Go on. Any details?"

"Just that there were incendiary bombs planted with radio receivers that would set them off on signal."

"What kind of signal?"

Moon looked puzzled. Her face wrinkled. "Gee, I think it had something to do with—oil wells? I don't know."

"Oil wells," muttered Juarez.

"Forget that," said Mace. "Go on."

"The point is, Mr. Galey wanted to send the signal immediately. But the Major wanted confirmation from Peking. Apparently his orders were to coordinate the bombing with Peking's moves. Something like that."

"And?"

"The upshot of it was that the Major wanted to wait and Mr. Galey vowed to blow the incendiaries in the morning."

"Why in the morning?"

"I don't know," Moon said.

"In the morning," Juarez repeated.

"How was he going to send the signal?" Mace asked.

Moon shook her head. "I don't know. It didn't make any sense to me."

"What else?"

"That's all. Actually, I was stunned, listening to all this. I'm a member of the Social Affairs Department, but I didn't want to do anything like what the

Major was planning! Mr. Galey never told me about that. We were just trying to present our ideas to the public on the KHOU-TV programming. That kind of thing. Propaganda."

Mace nodded. "Okay, Moon. What happened then?"

"Well, Nicky Grasso wasn't really knocked out, even though I hit him with a chair. He came crawling along the corridor, and he heard what Mr. Galey and the Major were talking about. And he threatened to shoot them—telling me to get away, that he'd rescue me. And he tried to kill the Major."

"Go on."

"The Major kicked his gun away, in one of those Kung Fu moves you use, Vic."

Mace's brows rose. So the Major was a Kung Fu expert, was he? Meeting him would be very interesting.

"What about Galey?" Juarez asked.

"When the Major took care of Nicky, Mr. Galey came after me, but I outran him. It was dark outside. And when I got to you and the gardener, Mr. Galley couldn't even see me any more."

Juarez shrugged. "That's it, then. Do you remember anything more about that incendiary device?"

"Nothing." Moon frowned. "I'm trying to remember what it was all about. An oil well. That was it. No! An oil well—lighter! An oil well lighter—that's what Mr. Galey said."

"Oil well lighter," muttered Juarez.

Mace rose, staring out the window into the night. "Those damned oil well cigarette lighters Petroleum Institute sends out."

"Jesus," said Juarez.

"That's how they're going to do it," Mace said, turning. "Don't you see? There's a radio transmitter

176

inside each one of those. It picks up a master signal and then sends it on to the incendiary bomb. The incendiary bombs obviously can't pick up signals from any great distance. And the lighters control the distribution of the secondary signals."

"But where is the primary signal coming from?" Juarez pondered.

"It's got to be pretty powerful to reach all over the country where those lighters are. Hell, P.I. has sent those out to every oil installation in the States!"

"What do we do? Go all over the country and destroy the lighters?"

"We don't have time to contact every owner to get rid of them. You heard what Galey's H hour is. Tomorrow morning." Mace frowned suddenly. "Of course!"

"Of course—what?" Juarez wondered.

Moon said, "What do you mean, Vic?"

"But that's it, you see. He *has* to wait until morning."

"To send the signal?" Juarez frowned.

"Right."

"Why?" Moon asked.

"He's got to get into the right place to send it."

"You mean the signaling device isn't in his own home?" Juarez asked. "I'd of course assumed it must be there. We were going to destroy the house to get at it."

"It's not there," Mace said positively. "Don't you see?"

"No," said Moon.

Mace smiled. He stood up. "Moon, you stay here. No one will bother you. Benny, you and I are going to get some sleep. We've got a lot of work to do in the morning."

"In the morning?"

"Before the sun comes up."

"What do we do?"

"We see that the signal doesn't go out."

Juarez frowned and looked at Moon. She was simply staring at Mace with a puzzled look.

"How?"

Juarez and Mace shrugged. Juarez sighed and went over to his black bag. He opened it and gazed inside.

"What'll you need?" he asked Mace.

"I'll need that electronics man," Mace answered. "Nothing else."

"Code name Sigma," said Juarez with a quick nod. "When does the operation go down?"

"Nine-ish. Bright and early."

"What's in the bag?" Moon asked, her eyes black with interest.

"Dirty tricks," said Mace.

Juarez opened the neck and Moon peered in. "Wires and more wires."

"What's that putty-like gook?" Moon pointed.

"Plastique. It's just clay. But it's made out of cyclonite and nitrocumene. You run a charge of electricity through that and you'll get one hell of an explosion."

"Gee," said Moon.

"Let's split," Mace suggested. "Moon, you stay here until the operation's wrapped up."

"Sure. I wouldn't want to get in your way."

CHAPTER THIRTEEN

Hank Shatford pulled up to the curb and left the engine running. In a split second he was inside the phone kiosk, dialing.

"Danny?"

Bolton's sleepy voice answered. "Yeah?"

"I picked up Mace."

Bolton came immediately awake. "Where?"

"Out in Fairbanks. Juarez's place. He's going down U.S. 290 with Juarez now."

"Follow them."

"But, Danny—"

"Follow them!" yelled Bolton. He hung up.

Shatford jumped out of the booth and got in the car, trying to edge out into the traffic and pick up the sight of Juarez's minibus at the same time. He was cursing Bolton and the drivers around him as he continued to maneuver into the fast lane.

At 8:45 Juarez picked up the car telephone and rang into the pod.

"Pod," said Quinn.

"Any news?"

"Giraffe is on the way to the Target Area. Falcon may be with him."

"Good."

The guard at the garage elevator doors to Tom Galey's private penthouse suite in the General Jackson Building smiled as the Cadillac pulled into its proper spot and settled down with a sigh.

Galey got out. So did Major Fong. The guard's eyes narrowed at the sight of the ugly and coarse Chinese. But he smiled nevertheless at Galey.

"Good morning, sir."

"Hello Albert. Everything secure?"

"Tight as a drum!"

Galey smiled broadly. "Good, Albert. Good! Now don't let anyone up in this shaft. No matter *what* happens here. Got that?"

The guard frowned. "Of course, sir. Nobody ever got past me yet."

"Perhaps because no one ever tried hard before," Galey observed. The guard looked puzzled.

The elevator doors opened and Galey followed Major Fong inside. The guard watched the lights on the long thin strip. The elevator arrived at the top and the lights blinked out.

"Mr. Galey?"

"Yes, Miss Wright."

"There's a Detective Captain Dekker on the phone."

"What does he want?"

"He won't say."

"Put him on. I've only just come in, but I'll talk to him."

"Thank you, sir."

"Mr. Galey?" Dekker's heavy voice intoned.

"That's right. What can I do for you, Captain Dekker?"

"It's about an employee of yours. A Miss Lingdoo."

"Yes?"

"I'm afraid I've got to ask you some questions."

"I'm terribly busy this morning, Captain and—"

"I don't mind. I'll be right over."

"I'm afraid that won't be possible, Captain. I'm working on a brand new programming breakdown for the summer months."

"I'll be there in fifteen minutes."

"Well, I suppose—"

"See you then!"

It was 9:03. Juarez sat in the minibus with Mace. Juarez was on the phone.

"Pod," said Quinn.

"What's new?"

"I've got a message from Grackle. He's across the street from the General Jackson Building."

"Yes?"

"There's a big limo crawling down into the underground parking lot—Galey's private area."

"What kind of limo?"

"City markings. It's a police unmarked. Captain Dekker is in the back seat."

Juarez smiled. "Captain Dekker?"

"That's what Grackle says."

Mace climbed down the steps into the basement proper of the General Jackson Building. He was observed by a tall thin man in coveralls. Across the back of the tall thin man's clothing were the words APEX ELEVATOR. Mace nodded.

"I'm Theta," said Mace.

"I'm Sigma."

Mace looked around and spotted the tool box near the elevator door. "Is this mine?"

"Right." Sigma pulled another box out of a pile of crates in the corner. "Let's go."

They stood in front of the elevator and pushed the button. In a moment the elevator came and they got in. The doors closed behind them. It said MAINTENANCE across the front.

An armed guard paced in front of the high broadcasting towers on top of the General Jackson Building. He was bored, but he knew he could not sit down or loaf. He knew that Mr. Galey had a surveillance team at all times posted in a suite of rooms in the Exxon Building across the way, watching.

The second guard was standing in the shadow of the elevator machinery shack, which was a metal building not far from the tower. A tool shed and general operations shack were located across the way.

The armed guard pulled out a walkie-talkie.

"It's Jake. Calling in. Everything okay."

"Roger," said a voice.

The other guard by the shack pulled out his own walkie-talkie and said: "It's Ken. Calling in. No problems."

"Dekker," said the big rock-faced man. "Captain of Detectives."

The elevator guard shook his head. "Mr. Galey don't want nobody upstairs."

"He wants me. Give him a call." Dekker pointed to the elevator phone.

After a moment's thought, the guard nodded and lifted the phone. "Mr. Galey? There's a Captain Dekker down here. He says—"

He listened. Then he nodded.

"Yes sir. No one else after him. Right." He hung up and stared at Dekker. "You can go on up. But first, I've got orders to frisk you."

Dekker grinned. He lifted his hands. "I'm clean, punk."

The guard flushed, and began patting him down.

"Weird way to get your kicks," Dekker observed, and the guard punched the elevator button as if it might be Dekker's chin.

The man seated in the parked Chrysler Imperial on Interstate 45 came up with a start that almost cracked his forehead against the windshield. He grabbed for the car phone.

"Pod!"

Yeah," said Quinn.

"It's the broad. The Chinese. She's leaving the motel."

"What?"

"Yeah. Hey—there's a car waiting. It's a rental— Hertz job! She's getting in it!"

"Tail her," snapped Quinn.

The free-lance contract agent for the C.I.A. got the Chrysler going and zoomed out into traffic. Right into the line of cars, he thought wearily. Right back into Houston!"

Captain Dekker came out of the elevator on the twenty-first floor of the General Jackson Building. In front of him stood two guards who could have been brothers to the man who had let him into the elevator in the basement after a short hassle.

"You don't mind?" asked the first of the twin guards, reaching out to pat him down.

Dekker grinned and raised his arms. "Boy, you guys are efficient."

The guard said nothing. He worked over Dekker's clothes carefully. No wires. No weapons. The second guard waited and when the first was finished, he too went over Dekker's body.

"Clean."

The first guard turned and inserted a slotted plastic rectangle into a slit in the door. A red light buzzed after a moment. Then the door opened automatically.

Dekker passed through, smiling thoughtfully at the elaborate display of security.

Tom Galey was seated at a massive desk at the far end of a long room that resembled a tennis court without a net in the center.

"Captain Dekker?" Galey asked with a faint smile.

"Mr. Galey? It's about your employee, Miss Lingdoo. I think she's been involved in murder. And she's disappeared."

Galey's face was expressionless. "Well, then, by all means arrest her. We have a reputation to maintain here. But be sure she is guilty before you pick her up, Captain."

Dekker flushed. "See here—"

Mace waited for the elevator to stop. The light under 20 went on. The doors opened. He waved to Sigma. Sigma went out into the corridor, carrying his tools. There was a stairwell to the right of the maintenance elevator. ROOFTOP, it said.

They climbed the stairs and Sigma punched a key into the locked door. It opened. They walked out onto the roof of the twentieth floor. The sun was bright, but the day was not yet as hot as it was going to be.

On the roof Mace stared at two of the sheds that rose above the surface of the flat area. One was the elevator machinery shack. The other was a shed of tools and window washing equipment. The window washers used the roof for the higher floors, from which they ran down the scaffolding. Other elevator machinery shacks were in the form of a shed along the back of the building.

Sigma put another key into the door to the elevator housing. The door opened. Mace walked inside. Sigma stayed out.

One of the guards on the twenty-first floor roof sauntered over to the edge and peered down at Sigma. He was holding his rifle. Sigma turned and waved at him.

"Morning!"

The guard said nothing.

A second man appeared on the roof by the first. He too held his rifle at the ready.

"Morning," said Sigma again.

Finally the first guard grunted a reply. "What in hell's wrong?"

"Nothing," said Sigma cheerily. "Maintenance elevator's 'got some bug in it. The rest are okay." Sigma waved to the elevator machinery shed along the line of the roof.

"Uh," said the second guard.

Inside the elevator's machinery room Mace was watching out through the narrow dirty window. He could see the two guards. The sun was behind them and they presented excellent targets. Noiselessly he eased the small window open. Fastening two pieces of wood and a string together, he bolted a small crossbow in place and quickly inserted an arrow head tipped not with a steel arrow but with a hypodermic needle. He aimed and shot the second guard in the side. The guard crumpled to the roof, backwards, in a heap. The other guard turned in astonishment. Then, realizing something was wrong, he lifted the rifle and aimed at Sigma. Mace shot

185

him in the arm with the second hypodermic arrow
and he too sank to the roof.

Hank Shatford waved at Danny Bolton in the
parking lot outside the General Jackson Building.
Bolton climbed out of the car and puffed over to
Shatford's car.

"Mace is in there." Shatford pointed.

"The General Jackson Building?" Bolton frowned.

"Yeah. See the car?"

He pointed to the minibus.

"Who's with him?"

"Juarez."

"Juarez went in with him?"

"They both went in the back door."

"Who's in the building?"

"Lots of people."

"I don't get it."

"You know your friend Captain Dekker?"

"Yeah."

"He's in there too."

Bolton stared. "Who's he visiting?"

"He went into the basement parking lot. That
means he was going in to see Tom Galey."

"Tom Galey?"

"He runs the Public Broadcasting Station."

"What in hell's that?"

"KHOU-TV."

"Why's Dekker interested in him?"

"Who knows."

"Hold it! Hold it! We did a film Public Broadcasting showed once."

"Who did a film?"

"We. Petroleum Institute."

"So?" Shatford wasn't impressed.

"I delivered the damned thing to Galey. He's got a

Chinese secretary."

Shatford's eyebrows went up. "The Chinese broad who helped the Kung Fu bastard?"

Bolton snapped his fingers. "I'll just bet you it was—"

"You've got to go in the basement garage to get to Galey's. There's a guard."

"Did Mace go in through there?"

"No. He's in the *other* basement."

"You stay here. If I don't come out of Galey's in fifteen minutes, you come in fast and get me."

Immediately Mace pulled out the long lengths of catgut from the tool box he carried. These were *K'oli-Pak-Shis*, long strands of tough catgut with grappling hooks on the end. They had been developed in the Thirteenth Century by the Shao Lin *Tung-chias* for scaling walls and cliffs.

Mace rushed out onto the roof and whirled the catgut strands over his head, and then let them go. The grappling hooks grabbed into the tarpaper of the roof over the twenty-first floor, holding tight into the tarred joint between the roof and the six inch parapet that surrounded the roof.

Quickly Mace twisted the strands together and climbed up to the roof. He beckoned Sigma, and Sigma followed, scrambling up over the edge and running across to the elevator housing shack.

Mace pulled up the catgut lines and coiled them around his chest under his coveralls. Immediately he ran over to the maintenance shack behind Sigma. Sigma fitted the key in and the door opened. To the side of the machinery shack Mace could see the stair entrance leading down to the twenty-first floor. It was padlocked with a triple padlock. A steel bar had been affixed, welded to the metal fire door surface and to the metal door frame. The blues had been right about that mode of entry: no go. Mace reasoned that there was probably a similar steel clamp on the door downstairs.

"Here we go!" cried Sigma, and ducked inside the elevator machinery shack.

Captain Dekker leaned forward in his chair. He was looking Galey right in the eye. He didn't like the smooth talking young man, because he knew that Galey considered himself better than anybody else. But Dekker needed Galey.

"Look," the big cop said. "I can roll you up along with your whole operation if you don't cooperate."

Galey smiled faintly. "What is it you wish, Captain?"

"I want that Chinese bastard. Mace. I know who he is. We've penetrated the deep cover op he's working on. He's tied in with the Chinese girl who works for you. I want him for murder."

Galey shrugged. "How can I help you?"

"Where's the girl?"

"I don't know."

"Come on, Mr. Galey! You've got to do better than that! After all—"

The phone rang. Galey glanced at his telephone with surprise. He had ordered all calls surveilled. Then he saw that it was the hot line.

He lifted it, nodding to Captain Dekker.

The man on the twentieth floor of the Exxon Building on watch could not believe his eyes. He had seen the two guards on top of Galey's penthouse saunter over to the roof to look down onto the twentieth floor roof. And then, quite suddenly, the two men had simply vanished. One minute they were there—and the next they were gone! He picked up the hot line to Galey's office and rang the chief.

"Something's in the works on your roof, Mr. Galey."

"What is it, you fool?"

"I can't see too well. But the guards are both neutralized." He was holding the glasses tight to his eyes now, but he could not see clearly. He was facing the sun.

Moon Chu Lingdoo tooled the rented Hertz Chevy into the underground garage of the building whose every floor she knew by heart and parked beside a large Pontiac she did not recognize. There were only allowed personnel in the garage lot. She wondered who might own it. Shrugging, she stepped out of the car, slammed the door, and hurried over to the elevator.

It was at that moment she realized the guard was not there. She hesitated, and then moved forward, looking about curiously. As she did so a man stepped out from behind Galey's Cadillac.

"Oh, it's—"

She never finished. Bolton shoved the Smith and Wesson 9mm in her side, and gestured to the elevator. The doors were open. "Get in, kid."

Moon felt faint, but determined not to slump to the concrete floor. She glanced sideways at the big man and realized she had seen him before. He was the man who had been with Captain Dekker the night Mace had been set up at the Legion Temple.

Son of a bitch, she thought. What was this?

They got in the elevator, and as she turned around to watch the doors close, she could see the guard's form stretched out on the near side of the Cadillac.

189

She glanced at Bolton in terror, but he only smiled harshly.

The doors closed.

Bolton pushed the button. The elevator ascended swiftly. Moon clutched her bag tightly in her hand. She could feel the rounded edges of the lumpy clay inside the bag. It was a large square of plastique she had stolen from the C.I.A. man's gadget bag at the motel. She had a good use for it.

Sigma inserted the key in the door to the elevator machinery room and slipped inside. Mace followed him, closing the door tightly behind him. The electronics man removed a pair of insulated pliers from his tool chest and moved over to the panel containing the operating leads for the private elevator to Galey's penthouse.

Mace took the time to study the interior of the machinery room. He could see the big electric motor which ran the elevator. He knew from a study of the blueprints Juarez had given him that the power for the elevator resided in the machinery room right here. That included both the power and the ultimate control of the power.

Supplementary controls—the remote controls that worked from inside the elevator and from the ground floor panel—were all spliced in to this main panel and from the main panel they ran directly to the electric motor in the corner.

The elevator operation consisted of a drive sheave —a drive shaft with cogs over which elevator cables ran—and the motor itself. The remote control buttons in the elevator were connected to the signal panel by means of traveling cables that carried electric current from the main power source in the machinery room to the elevator itself for lights and for

the signaling mechanism. Other remote control buttons on the various floors ran up through the shaft to
the machinery room control panel.

The drive sheave ran from the motor out across
the center of the elevator shaft. Over this cogged
shaft a fascis of separate cables passed, attached at
one end to the top of the elevator cage and at the
other end to the counterweight—a heavy weight that
exactly balanced the weight of the cage plus forty
per cent of a full load of people.

An ordinary carload—balanced by the counterweight—was so nearly constant that it took only a
minimum of power to turn the drive sheave and
bring the elevator up or lower it. The controls for the
activation and deactivation of the drive shaft were
located in the panel which Sigma was now opening.

With the metal cover off the rectangular panel,
Mace could see a spaghetti-like cluster of colored
wires and splices that was a nightmare of electronics
wizardry. Sigma knew what he was doing, Mace was
sure. Let him make the alterations on the panel that
would freeze the elevator cage at the top and cut off
access or egress to and from Galey's penthouse.

Sigma studied the assemblage of wires for a moment and then leaned forward confidently, clipping
an orange wire and a blue one. Then he snipped
through a green and a white. He twisted these free
and respliced them in a different order. As he was
working, the drive sheave turned as the motor
hummed. Mace could hear the elevator come up in
the shaft. It stopped just below them. There were
voices and someone laughed.

Sigma went to work on the wires once again, working for several minutes. Then he checked over his
work visually and lifted his hand to flip a switch in
the corner of the panel. The elevator below them did
not move. Nor would it now. The twenty-first floor

191

was isolated. No one could either get in or get out without the use of the elevator, which was neutralized.

Sigma closed the control panel and waved a finger to Mace, pointing downward. Mace leaned over. Sigma's finger was indicating the floor of the machinery room. Mace saw a trapdoor in the center of it, near the slot through which the cables ran. Mace pulled the trap door open. He could see down to the cables hooked in the top of the elevator cage. He could see the top of the cage and the second trapdoor that now hung directly below the trapdoor in the machinery room.

Sigma nodded. Mace climbed down and stood on the top of the cage. He could feel it sway slightly. He leaned over and flipped at the butterfly bolts that held the trap in place. When the screws were removed the door lifted off easily. He pushed it aside and climbed down into the cage, dropping gracefully to the floor. He looked up to Sigma and waved his hand. Sigma nodded and flipped a switch. The doors in front of Mace opened.

Galey slammed down the phone and glanced across the room at Dekker. "What kind of goddamned monkey business are you pulling, Captain?"

Dekker was startled. His neck turned red. "Huh, me?"

"You! You can't arrest me!"

"I'm not going to bust you, Mr. Galey!" shouted Dekker in alarm. "Whatever gives you that idea?"

"Then what's going on around here?" Galey cried out, pushing his chair back and jumping to his feet. "The roof—"

The door to Galey's office opened and four guards

tepped inside, all armed, all pointing their hand-
guns at Dekker. Dekker turned and went white.
'What the hell is this?''

"Get your cops off my roof! I'll sue the shit out of
you, Dekker! You'll never work in any town in this
country after I'm through with you!"

"I don't know what the fuck you're talking
about!"

Galey made a signal to the guards. One of them
nodded and aimed at Dekker's gut.

Major Fong was frantically scrambling through
the books and papers and cans of inch-and-a-half
tape that littered the Log Room off Galey's office.
Galey had indicated that the transmission signal
was located in the Log Room when they had first
come into the office.

The Major had been searching frantically ever
since for it.

The affirmative call had come in shortly before
breakfast. Galey's night operator at the transmitter
in the office had telephoned it in to Galey's home.
Peking had affirmed the detonation of the incendiaries in a heavily coded message.

Major Fong was now looking for the transmission
signal to feed into the transmitter. Galey, who had
been about to send out the crucial signal, had been
interrupted to "take care" of the rather stolid type
now seated in the office. The visitor looked and
smelled like cop to Major Fong, who had had experi-
ence with the breed in China and Vietnam. What in
hell truck did Galey have with the law?

The Major cursed at the papers and rubble in the
Log Room. Galey hadn't had time to tell him where
the damned signal was. It might be in writing, it
might be in code, it might even be on film or on

tape. How in hell—?

Major Fong heard a loud noise outside. Galey ha
been speaking quietly with the big cop, but no
there was an interruption—a loud noise that sound
ed suspiciously like a door slamming.

No—it was a shot. Two shots!

Major Fong pushed open the door to the Lo
Room and looked out into the office.

Bolton grabbed Moon, holding her like a shield
He had gotten off the elevator, to the surprise of the
two guards who were waiting but not expecting ar
armed man to force his way through them with a familiar figure held as a shield. They knew Moon. Instinctively they let their guns down.

Bolton pushed Moon ahead of him, making for the
door to Galey's office.

"You can't go in there," said one of the guards
frantically. Bolton turned the 9mm S&W at the
man's stomach.

Moon was smiling. She kept gripping her handbag.

Bolton pushed on the door. It was locked. Moon
smiled mutely at the first guard. He removed the
plastic strip and inserted it in the lock slot. The door
opened automatically. Bolton saw the long room,
with Galey and Dekker at the end of it. He saw the
four guards who were as surprised as he was.

One of them wheeled and fired.

Bolton killed him. Moon screamed. Then Bolton
saw the Chinese man come hurtling out of a room at
the far end of the office. Galey yelled something at
the Chinese.

Victor Mace stepped out of the elevator and saw
the two armed guards whom Bolton had faced down.
One of them blinked his eyes at the sight of Mace,
unarmed, and raised the gun in his hand to fire.

194

Mace smiled to himself. It was so easy. As he went to work on the first two guards, he could see through the open door into the other room. He could see Galey, and Major Fong, and the four guards, one down, and Dekker and Bolton.

It was old home week.

Mace jumped.

CHAPTER FOURTEEN

Mateo Velasquez had been a guard for Tom Galey for two years on the day he confronted Victor Mace at the door into the boss's sanctum sanctorum. The orphan product of the stews of Lisbon, Portugal, Velasquez had stowed away in a merchant marine after World War II was over and as a youth had made his way in New York City by his knife and his wits, finally gravitating to St. Louis and on to Dallas and Houston. Now skilled in automatic weapons as well as side arms as a result of a short tour in Vietnam, Velasquez considered himself an excellent fighter.

But Mateo while able to live by his wits was not an intellect by any means. When events occurred which were not usual and when his way of life was abruptly torn out of its familiar pattern, he tended to fret and sulk and freeze.

The startling appearance of the Chinese girl who was Mr. Galey's secretary—*and* held like a shield in front of a big bruiser of a Texan with a red face and wild eyes—was a shock of prodigious proportions to Mateo Velasquez. She had appeared so quickly, and

the man holding her had seemed so deucedly domi-
neering, that Velasquez had been willing to oblige by
opening the door with the plastic strip.

Hardly had he turned from contemplation of the
rather interesting scene inside the office—into which
four other guards had just entered—than a noise at-
tracted his eye to the open elevator in front of him.
And emerging from the formerly *empty* elevator was
a tall limber-looking man with a Chinese cast to his
face.

Jesus, Mary and Joseph, Mateo muttered to himself. There was nothing for it but to act. The Chinese girl in the hands of a big man, the four guards
summoned by Mr. Galey, the big cop-like guy in
there talking to Mr. Galey, and that rough bruiser of
a Chinese looking like a rock crusher already in
there with the boss—it was just too much.

Mateo lifted the heavy Colt .45 caliber automatic
and squeezed the grip to fire. But he never got off
the shot. Like lightning, the Chinese type seemed to
soar off the floor like a goddamned bird, and came
at Velasquez in a sideways hop, left foot first, leg
stiffened out right at Velasquez's neck. Velasquez
tried to twist his arm and fire at the leg, but he
never got a chance.

Mace's *Yoko-tobi-geri* ball-of-the-foot kick to the
Portuguese's jaw threw him backward into the door
frame. Mace could hear the crack as the jaw shattered even before he bounced onto the floor, recover-
ing from the high kick. Then, as the guard's spine
smashed into the door frame, his vertebra was
snapped. Pain radiated from the fracture all over the
man's body, meeting the waves of nausea prompted
by the hanging and useless jawbones splintered by
Mace's kick. Velasquez sank in a dead faint, far
along the path toward death.

Bill Watson, who shared the duty with Velasquez

hat morning, had been utterly contemptuous of Velasquez's intimidation by the big Texan holding Mr. Galey's secretary, but he hadn't interfered. He never thought much of the spik's prowess with either his gun or his brain, but since Velasquez was his senior and since Velasquez had a raunchy disposition, Watson more or less let it go at that.

When he saw what the foreign-looking type did to Velasquez's jaw and face, he was moving before Mace got to the floor again. Realizing that the stopping power of the .45 caliber Colt that Mr. Galey had them wear in their duty assignments wasn't enough to stop this lithe, acrobatic fighter, Watson wielded the weapon like a club, aiming at Mace's head with the heavy grip end, slamming it toward the side of Mace's head.

Mace had seen Watson move as he came down from the high jump kick and twisted as he landed, throwing his head back out of range of the windmill blow and thrusting a deadly double knuckle shot in the solar plexus as the California-born guard swung at him.

The solar plexus blow sent Watson stumbling to one side, paralyzing his nerve centers. But Watson, eyes glazed, was not done yet. Mace was wheeling in even as Watson tried to react with a knee to the groin kick. Mace parried the kick with an *Uri Zuki* sweep-leg block, caroming Watson off his knee and onto the floor. Watson, still alert, raised the Colt to fire.

Mace leaped, taking a lung-full of air and screaming the Kung Fu attack: "KA-AI!"

Then he gave a high leap, and landed on the desperate Watson with a *Neko Ashi Dachoi*, a leaping double kick, to the high chest. Bones snapped. Splinters entered Watson's aorta and pierced the muscle sheath. His abdomen was ruptured by the force of the blow and he was bleeding internally as he flopped over on his back like a fish out of water.

Mace's cry had alerted everyone inside Tom Galley's office. He could see Bolton's huge form directly in front of him, with Dekker, the big police officer, beyond, near the large desk. He could see Galey moving forward beside the desk, and Major Fong in the background, solid and evil as a monster in a horror show.

Besides those he knew, Mace saw one man on the floor, and three others who could only be guards, waiting for him. Bolton was turning now, holding a smoking weapon in his hand. He saw Mace. Mace was surprised at the sight of Moon Chu Lingdoo in Bolton's arms. He stored that puzzling fact in his memory and began to analyze the situation in split second fashion as he ran through the doorway toward one of the guards.

Mace knew Bolton would fire. He aimed his line of attack in such a fashion that he would direct Bolton's eye to one specific spot. Then, as Bolton reacted exactly as anticipated, Mace twisted to the side and hurtled himself through the air toward the larger of the three guards who were spaced out and waiting to entrap him.

Roy Gant was the biggest man on Tom Galey's security staff. He was six feet seven, with an enormous body to match. He didn't carry an ounce of fat on his frame. He had been known to handle six men in a bar room brawl down in the old part of Houston. When he saw Mace come springing in through the doorway, Gant decided he wanted to take this man himself, and give him the old bear-hug smother-crush. He didn't like chinks anyway.

Gant hadn't drawn his gun. He advanced on Mace, big arms swinging at his sides, a behemoth out of prehistory. Mace came in effortlessly and swiftly, moving straight ahead after dodging the shot which Bolton threw into empty air. Before Bolton could readjust his aim and fire again, Mace moved in on Gant with a sweeping barrier block against Gant's big bear-arm stance, spun around sideways, and hit him in the left side near the heart with an elbow blow that made the giant suck in his air like a wounded animal, and then gave him a left-handed *Kagi-Zaki* hook punch to the chin.

Gant went over backward like a sequoia falling.

Bolton fired another shot. Mace was no longer there. He wheeled and struck out at the gunhand of the Petroleum Institute operative and slammed him in the chops with a *Haishu-Uchi* back of the hand strike which staggered him back and made him let go of Moon.

Then Mace recovered and slapped him in the ribs with an *Age Empi* front attack with the left elbow which broke a rib and sent Bolton reeling sideways. With his right hand he executed a knuckle blow to the carotid artery and blacked out Bolton so that he slumped to the floor without further struggle.

The remaining guards were running out into the hallway. They didn't want any more of this Oriental whirlwind. Mace made an instant survey of the office and found Galey bent over the desk obviously going for a weapon of some kind. The big police officer, Captain Dekker, had picked up Bolton's dropped side arm and was watching Mace carefully.

Mace read Dekker. He knew Dekker was aware of Mace's abilities. He knew also that Dekker wanted him for the homicides on the oil drilling rig. Dekker wanted Mace alive so he could parade him in front of media cameras for top publicity. Mace read Dekker's intention to wound Mace and carry him back to interrogate and try and hang under the camera lights. Therefore Dekker would not shoot to kill.

Galey would. Mace could see that Galey had got hold of something in a desk drawer and was rising now, pushing himself around in back of it for cover. For some reason Galey thought Mace was armed. Mace almost laughed. Moon was on the floor, playing possum. She was watching Mace through half-closed eyes. Major Fong was moving slowly toward Mace, his face frozen in a ghastly grin.

Mace used Dekker as a shield between him and Galey. He moved toward Dekker slowly, watching him very carefully. Dekker's face was impassive. He held the gun solidly in his hand and lifted it to cover Mace's chest. Still, Mace did not think he would fire.

Behind Dekker, Mace could see Galey trying to get around in position to fire at Mace without hitting the big cop. Mace simply altered his path to keep the line of fire eclipsed by Dekker's body. It was not intuition, it was his very careful analysis of Dekker's aims and a perfect study of his moves that gave Mace his chance.

Dekker's cheek twitched at the precise moment he shifted stance. Mace could see the weight shift in Dekker's body. Mace knew he was going to move forward and somehow use his right foot. Instantly Mace reasoned that Dekker would kick at Mace's crotch. The groin was the most vulnerable spot in any man's body for a forward-under attack.

Mace's eyes shifted to Dekker's right foot. The knee lifted, the foot swung back and then began its forward trajectory as Dekker swung his body back at the waist to balance the kick.

The Kung Fu master instantly stepped back into a combination of the *Tiger Stretches Its Paws* stance, turning his body away from the coming kick by pivoting to the right on the right knee, and lowering the left hand in a *Lo-Mar Dzi-Nar,* Tiger Claw

ow Block, smashing at Dekker's ankle top with the
eel of the left hand. The force of the blow spun
Dekker off target and staggered him slightly.

Mace swiftly twisted the other way and came in
oward Dekker's throat with his right hand in an
open hand *Nukite* strike to Dekker's breast bone.
Off balance, Dekker stumbled and almost went
down. Mace added to the obvious momentum with a
left-handed roundhouse blow to the side of the neck.
Dekker fell to the floor, stunned.

With Dekker's body out of the way Galey could
fire. He took careful aim and spun off a shot at
Mace.

Back in the minibus Benny Juarez was on the
phone. It was Plato, patched in through the pod by
Quinn.

"There's something funny going on," Plato said.
"Dekker's left. He's in the General Jackson Building
interrogating Tom Galey."

"I'm in the back lot. We know he's here."

"There's more. A back-up group of six of Dekker's
plainclothes detectives has gone out there now.
They're going up to back Dekker's play."

"What *is* Dekker's play?"

"He may be going to bust Galey."

"For what?"

"The rubouts at the Chinese girl's pad."

Juarez whistled. "You come out here. We're going
up. Mace is here too."

"On the way."

The big Packard swerved down the ramp and almost smashed into the concrete wall as it swerved to
a stop. The six men climbed out quickly and ran

over to the elevator doors in the corner.

"You know the play," said the leader, a tough forty-five year old pro named Stacy Keene. "We go up in the elevator and we break through the guards. Gino, you take the guard at the door here."

Gino Massiccio pointed to the elevator. "Nobody there."

Keene blinked. He led the group over to the elevator doors. He was the one who found the guard lying crumpled up beside the Cadillac owned by Tom Galey.

"Jesus Christ," said Gino. "He's in bad shape."

"Somebody else got in ahead of us," said Keene. "Ring for the elevator, will you, Bateman?"

Bateman punched the button. Nothing happened.

"Shit," said Keene. "Somebody sabotaged the goddamned elevator. What the hell we gonna do?"

"Go into the main building and get off at twenty. Then we walk up." That was Fritzy Keitel.

"There's no stairs," said Keene. "Didn't you look at the blues?"

"Take the roof on twenty and climb up."

"What about the guards?" Bateman asked.

"Zap them. Let's go. You know what Dekker told us about this bunch. If they resist, wipe them out."

Plato and Juarez grabbed the maintenance elevator and got to the roof the same way Mace and Sigma had gone in three minutes after Plato had arrived at the General Jackson Building.

"Boost me," snapped Juarez, pointing to the wall.

Plato nodded and clenched his hands together in a stirrup for Juarez's foot. Juarez jumped up into the stirrup and stretched as high as he could. He grabbed the parapet.

"Christ, you're heavy," said Plato.

"It's all chili and tamales," grunted Juarez.

Plato groaned.

The door to the stairwell opened and someone shouted across the open roof.

"Freeze, you bastards! Police!"

Plato stared across the roof, still holding Juarez as Juarez dangled from the parapet in the act of pulling himself up.

"What the fuck?" groaned Plato. "Stacy Keene!"

Keene was pulling his piece and running hard as he made out Plato, whom he knew as Francois Lafitte.

"Franky! What in hell—! I almost whiffed you."

Dekker's group poured out onto the roof. It began to look like a parade ground during smoke-if-you-got-them time.

"Jesus," said Lafitte. "Who's minding the store?"

"How'd Dekker get in touch with you?" Keitel wondered, coming up and staring at Juarez hanging from the parapet.

"He didn't," said Lafitte. "Hey, this is Juarez. Benny Juarez."

"Yeah," said Stacy Keene. "The head spook. What's coming down, some deep cover ops, Franky?"

Lafitte shrugged. "We got a wanted inside. Name's Galey."

"Dekker is in there. He wants Galey too."

"Well, hell, let's not just talk, let's move."

Juarez was still hanging. "Will you give me a goddamned boost, Franky? My arms are coming out."

Lafitte pushed hard with his hands and Juarez shot upward until he was folded over the parapet on his chest. He scrambled over, legs waving like a half-sick beetle in a fumigation raid.

He leaned over and reached down. "Jump, you bastards. Come on. Up. Up. Time's awasting."

Hank Shatford looked at his watch. Bolton had been gone for twenty minutes. Shatford bit his lip. He hated to have to go in and bail out his boss. Anyway, he didn't think too much of Bolton. The boss was pulling something cute that wasn't really straight. He knew that. And the boss wasn't letting Shatford get a suck at the sugar titty either. Bolton was probably mixed up with Captain Dekker and the guys Galey hired to do his dirty work in some bloody payoff.

He sighed. In a minute he was in the garage and crossing the floor. When he found the elevator wasn't working he glanced around and saw the guard who had been decked beside the Caddy. He punched the elevator button. Nothing. It looked like Bolton was probably in trouble up there, since Galey obviously had the elevator turned off.

Shatford walked around into the front of the General Jackson Building just as Stacy Keene and five dicks from H.P.D. converged on the elevators. Shatford pulled his hat around and gazed with intense interest at a mirror by the side of the newsstand. He watched the fuzz troop into the elevator. He watched the tiny stars on the elevator indicator light up at the twentieth floor.

Shatford walked over to another elevator and got in. At the twentieth floor he got out, looked up and down, and couldn't make out where the thundering herd had gone. He was at the end of the corridor trying to puzzle it out when he heard the shout of voices coming down from the stairwell marked ROOFTOP.

He took the steps two at a time.

And there was Juarez, the Mexican spook, and the cops, all scaling the wall to the penthouse roof like a swarm of ants on a sugar cube.

206

Tom Galey fired.

Mace had begun his forward dive at the same instant. The slug whizzed over his head. Galey immediately compensated and fired again. But Mace's low dive had given him plenty of momentum. He slid across the slick floor on his belly, coming all the way to the end of the desk. Quickly gripping the under edge and flipping himself up in a crouch to shield his body from Galey's line of fire, Mace moved with all the speed he could around to the right, which was a change of direction to fool Galey's firing eye.

He did. Galey waited with the gun pointed at the floor—on the opposite side of the desk. Mace quickly rose and arched his body, leaping across the desk with his two hands extended outward toward Galey's body. His hands were curved in the traditional *Lo-Mar Dzi-Nar* Tiger Claw strike posture, the middle fingers curved like the claws of a cat.

The Kung Fu Master's knee touched the desk top, supporting him as he extended his body and clutched at Galey's head, his right hand up with the fingers downward, his left hand down with the fingers upward.

As he sailed at Galey, Galey turned toward him, startled almost out of his wits. He was slow in bringing the gun in his hand around to squeeze off a shot at Mace. That hesitation was his undoing.

The Tiger Claw fingers struck Galey in the eyes with the up hand and in the throat with the down hand. The up hand ripped both Galey's eyeballs out of their sockets, tearing the flesh around them and popping them out onto his cheeks where they hung in blood and body fluid. The down hand slicked through Galey's throat muscles, removing the sheath

207

around the windpipe and leaving a tiny hole through which a thin stream of air rushed out of his chest.

Galey fell backward, the pain washing through him in waves. Eyes destroyed, neck torn, he was bathed in his own blood from the hit and rip of Mace's nails. He screamed out loud in a gurgle as he went over, flailing out with his right hand for support. The 9 mm. Luger he held slapped the floor.

Mace dove onto Galey's body. Blinded, unable to draw in a full breath of air through his destroyed throat, Galey nevertheless kicked gamely upward with his knee, trying to smash Mace's testicles. Mace bounded over in a quick somersault, bounced to his feet in a crouch, and faced his antagonist.

Galey swung to one side, trying to get to his feet. Blood poured out of his eyes and throat. He had his gun again; he whipped it around. "Where the hell are you?" he cried in rasping agony.

Mace leaped from a mini *Shiko Dachi* stance toward the dying man, doubling his fist and smashing him on the head with the *Tettsui-Uchi*, a hammer-hand dragon blow. Galey sank back, kicking up with his feet in an agony of effort. He caught Mace in the hips and flung him over his head onto the floor beyond.

Half stunned, Mace rolled to one side and rose to his knees, facing his pain-maddened opponent. Galey was crawling, rolling over, rising again, crouching, hands moving blindly in front of him in groping, clutching motions, trying to touch his tormentor's body, trying to rip out his reproductive organs if only he could find them.

Mace grabbed Galey's right arm with a *Kilu-Gocha* twist to the outward, breaking the wrist bone. Galey screamed as loud as his failing voice would permit, only a gurgle of escaping air now, and fell to one side. With his right hand dangling, he crawled toward Mace, left hand clawed out, searching for Mace's ankle.

The grip and twist was so ferocious it pulled Mace off his feet and dumped him on his head.

His left foot, freed mercifully, slammed at Galey's bloodied head, and Galey slid across the floor and lay there in hissing dissonance, twitching slightly, sinking into gory death. Mace rose. He turned to find Moon. She was gone.

The moment he saw the Kung Fu Mon-Master enter the office so swiftly and so confidently, Major Hsung Fong glanced at Captain Tom Galey for a quick decision. Galey made it.

"Send the detonator signal. Two slash four slash seventy-five air check tape. The transmitter is in the store room." The words were quick and in Chinese. Instantly Major Fong understood and vanished into the Log Room where the scripts and transmitter tapes for KHOU-TV were stored.

The hell with Peking, the Major thought. For once Galey was right. The cops were there, the Chinese Kung Fu expert, and even the guards and the S.A.D. girl. Galey had his hands full. It was up to Major Fong to send the signal, activate the oil well transmitter-detonators, and blow the incendiaries. Complete the mission—*then* figure out how to get out of this mess.

Quickly Major Fong flipped through the books and papers he had pulled from the shelves onto the work table. Two slash four slash seventy-five. Either second of April, 1975, or fourth of February, 1975. Was it month first, or day first as in the international system of doctrine? Damn the Americans for not knowing how to write dates! What he had to do was locate the air check for that day, slap it into the tape deck in the transmitter room, and turn on the machine.

On the way down Galey had explained to the Major that the radio transmitter he was going to use was rigged as a dummy *inside* the regular television transmitter on the roof of the General Jackson Building. And the control room for the special signal transmitter tower was in the store room at the back of the Log Room.

But where was two slash four slash seventy-five? Major Fong cursed and climbed up on a chair, flipping through the big cans of tape on the top shelf. He could hear a scream of anguish from the room outside. He had to hurry. Three slash eight slash seventy-five. Goddamn—

When Moon saw Mace come in through the doorway she instantly knew that everything was under control. Even though Galey had a gun and even though Bolton was armed, she knew that Mace could control them. But he could not control Major Fong.

Moon watched the Major as he darted back into the Log Room after the short exchange of words with Galey. She understood the words. Galey was telling Major Fong where the special detonator signal was located. It would be stored in the February fourth air check tape. And Moon also heard the last piece of information. The transmitter was in the store room.

It all fell into place for Moon. She had never been allowed in the store room. Mr. Galey had said it was filled with personal and private material. But of course it wasn't at all. That was the control room for the transmitter that Mr. Galey was going to use to send the special signal all over the country. Perhaps the transmitter was wired to the television tower. She didn't stop to think about that.

Mace was working on Dekker now. Moon crawled toward the far end of the room. There was a second entrance to the Log Room away from the point where Major Fong had gone in. She pushed open the door and closed it quietly. At the other end of the long room filled with shelves and heaped-up tins of tape she could hear Major Fong breathing heavily and cursing as he pulled down can after can, dropping the lids on the floor.

Moon saw the door marked STORE ROOM. She pushed the piles of scripts and story boards aside and tried the door. It was open!

She pushed in.

The small room was dark and smelled very oily, almost as if it were an engine room of some kind. There would be an electric motor in the transmitter, of course, she realized belatedly. There was a desk lamp with a goose neck shade pointing down onto a shiny formica table top. Behind the table top rose a bank of dials, instrumentation and tape dials—the console of a radio transmitter.

Moon flipped the wall switch at the door. The goose neck lamp went on.

A cone of light glared down on the formica. The dials in front of the operator's chair were clearly marked. ON. WAVE LENGTH. POWER. And so on.

Quickly Moon traced the lamp cord. It was plugged into a wall outlet not far from the wall switch. The switch at the door controlled the wall outlet; it turned on the lamp plugged into it.

Moon reached into her bag and brought out a pair of small cuticle scissors. She reached around and snapped off the light. It was dark in the small cubbyhole. She didn't have much time. She cut the lamp cord an inch from the base of the gooseneck lamp, and pulled away the plastic insulation, baring

211

the wires. Then she fumbled in her bag and got out the lump of plastique she had taken from the C.I.A. station officer's black bag and stuck the lump down on the side of the transmitter, out of sight of the doorway. Then she poked the two bare wires into the clay-like substance.

As she turned to leave she heard footsteps approaching the door to the store room. In terror she pressed herself against the wall. The steps were those of Major Fong—she could tell by the ponderous weight of them and the stolid tread.

The knob rattled and the door opened.

"Who's in there?" Major Fong's voice asked.

Moon trembled. A hand snaked in, groping for the light switch.

It didn't take Detective Stacy Keene long to locate the open door in the elevator machinery shack. Gino Massiccio had already found the ROOFTOP stairwell, which was padlocked. By that fact, Keene knew that no one had forced his way in through the stairs. He, or they, had chosen an easier and more secret way to effect surprise entry. Through the elevator machinery shack! He barged into the crowded space and saw the trap door open on the floor. He peered down through both openings into the elevator, into the startled eyes of a man looking up. Instantly that man—one of the two guards who had run away from Mace—raised the heavy Smith and Wesson in his hand and banged off a shot at Keene.

Keene threw himself to one side as the bullet smashed into the ceiling of the elevator machinery shack, damned near blowing the roof off. The reverberations of the shot stunned him, deafened him, and made him come up off the floor cursing. Another shot followed. Down below in the elevator the second guard was crying out to his buddy to cut it out, his eardrums had burst.

Gino Massiccio pushed past Keene, stuck his own piece down through the opening and blasted away until he had emptied every shot in his Colt .38 and a .45 frame Service Revolver into the aperture below.

There was silence.

"Who the hell were they?" Gino asked as he reached into his belt and brought out six short rounds to reload.

Keene shook his head. The other four detectives were staring blankly at Gino. Behind them Keene made out Juarez and Lafitte. Keene swaggered to his feet. "I'm going down into the elevator. Captain Dekker's in there somewhere."

He jumped down and swung onto the top of the elevator, then lowered himself into the cage below. The heavy odor of cordite filled the air, made his eyes water. The elevator doors were closed. He turned up and yelled at Gino.

"Give me a hand. We got to pry these damned doors open."

Gino climbed down. So did three more cops. In a moment they were sweating and cursing and wrenching at the closed doors.

Juarez came and peered down. The last of the detectives stood over Juarez looking past his shoulder.

Behind him a figure appeared, holding a small electrician's pliers. Sigma, who had kept out of sight at the appearance of the fuzz, taped the last detective on the side of the skull and the detective went down in a heap.

Juarez winked. Lafitte stood in the doorway with his hands on his hips. Juarez gestured to Sigma, pointing downward. Sigma lifted the cover from the control panel and punched a button, then twisted a switch. They could hear the powerful electric motor

213

come to life beside them. The power sheave turned. The elevator slowly descended toward the garage. There were shouts of surprise in the cage. Someone banged on the door.

Juarez watched through the trap door. Finally the elevator came to rest in the basement. At a signal from Juarez, Sigma flipped one of the switches. The doors whirred open. There was a cry of triumph. The elevator emptied out, except for the two bodies of Galey's guards. Then Sigma flipped another switch and the doors closed once again. The elevator rose quickly to the top floor where it had been before. Juarez jumped down onto the top and lowered himself into the elevator. Lafitte followed. Sigma pulled the first switch again.

The doors opened.

"Moon!" called Mace, gazing all around him in the large office. "Moon!"

There was no answer. He could hear vague cries in the distance, and the sound of the elevator grinding along in the shaft.

Major Fong was in the Log Room. Mace could see the letters on the door at the far end of the office. He ran across to it and tore it open. There were piles of paper and tins of film and tape everywhere. The room was in a shambles. As he stood there, gazing about in hasty scrutiny, he was aware of a sound at his right. Wheeling, he stood at the ready, facing the corner. It was a feint.

Instantly he heard the chuckle behind him. He had never heard Major Fong chuckle, but he had imagined how he would sound, and the laughter he now heard fitted the pattern in his mind. The Chinese S.A.D. officer was amused because he had thrown an object into the corner to distract Mace.

Swiftly Mace moved, but he was not quick enough.

There was a sound of toppling cans and sliding papers and before he could duck forward, he felt his neck in the crook of Major Fong's right arm, which was gripping him tightly. The Major had come from the direction of the store room door at the far left end of the Log Room.

Mace pulled downward, sagging with his knees touching the floor. Major Fong's left hand clasped his right, and both arms tightened their squeeze on Mace's neck. He could feel the pressure on his carotid artery and he began to see black around the edges of his vision.

He turned on his left knee, keeping his head close to Major Fong's biceps to reduce the pressure on his neck. Then, quickly, using his left knee as a springboard, Mace swung his bunched left fist upward in a short blow to the testicles. Major Fong grunted and a great whoosh of air left his lungs, blowing down on Mace's hair. Mace felt the Major's grip loosen. The left arm swung away, rising to strike downward.

Mace shot his right hand upward in a stunning three-fingered claw grab to the throat. But Major Fong knew the move, and backed away just enough to let Mace's fingers go harmlessly by.

Yet Mace had broken free from the neck grip. He twisted around, trying to gauge the close quarters in which he found himself more accurately to make the site itself contribute to his attack and defense.

He found Major Fong again one step ahead of him. The giant Chinese hill bandit had grabbed up a long piece of wood which Mace realized was a broken table leg two and a half feet long. It was round at one end and square and broken at the other.

The Major gripped the rounded end and wielded

the broken splintered working edge, aiming it at Mace's head. Mace reacted instinctively, as his years of training as a Kung Fu Master had taught him. He moved backward on his left leg, extending his right knee upward on the toes, his hands in claws and waving up and down at Major Fong.

"The classic stance," muttered Major Fong in Chinese.

"You are versed in the martial arts," Mace replied, watching carefully.

Major Fong laughed and as he did so, swung the table leg in a roundhouse blow from right to left, aiming at Mace's left ear. Mace dropped quickly to the floor, his left knee bending until it almost touched, and his right swerving to the outside. As Major Fong smashed the table leg into a shelf on the wall, the shock of the blow made the walls vibrate.

Mace settled on his backside, horizontal, and swung around until his feet were in position. Then he pulled them back and snapped both feet upward with the heels aimed directly at Major Fong's genitals in a *Gyokku-Ryu* double-legged piston kick.

Major Fong was startled, but recovered and launched himself in a flying leap over and past Mace's kicks. Mace had such power going that he continued the *Gyokku-Ryu* with a leap to his feet, whirling around and facing Major Fong.

"Not yet, my friend," said Major Fong with a flat and sinister smile.

"Soon," Mace rejoined, leaping forward.

Major Fong slapped to the side with a tremendous *Shotu-Uchi* blow that had an elbow-snapping momentum behind it, aimed at Mace's head. Mace slid under it and came at the Major with a *Gorii* push-slam-kick to the stomach.

The Major switched his body—quickly for a man his size and weight—and neutralized the blows.

216

Mace countered with a stabbing blow to the center of Major Fong's throat. The Major slapped down on Mace's head with stiff-handed *Nukite* stabs to the windpipe, which Mace avoided with an *Age-Uki* block, pushing Major Fong's stabs away and then turning his hip into the Major's body and throwing him into the wall with a jarring jolt.

The Major bounced off, his face mottled with rage. He was angry now. His eyes blazed at Mace.

"Now I kill," he hissed in Chinese.

"Try me," snapped Mace in English.

Major Fong launched a wide-swinging roundhouse kick to Mace's chest, which Mace defended with a *Kensetsu-Geri* stamping kick defense at the middle level.

Mace turned and leaped high in the air, extending his left foot in a *Mae-Tobi-Geri* aimed at the Major's head. The Major whipped back and avoided the attack, coming back with a *Gyaku-Zuki* reverse punch with the fist in Mace's chest.

The Kung Fu Master had failed to block the blow and went smashing down to the floor, his wind momentarily knocked out of him. Instantly the Major was on top of him, grinning, the sweat dripping off his chin onto Mace's face. The Major's hands were up and darting directly into Mace's eyes with a deadly *Nihon* two finger stab to the eyeballs.

Mace kicked hard with both knees in a double *Hiza Geri*, which caught the Major in the testicles. The Major cried out and smashed into the pile of film cans and Mace was up and on him, pinching hard at the pressure points in the neck. The Major's sternomastoid muscles swelled outward to reduce the pressure of Mace's grip.

Instantly Mace felt his ankle gripped with a band of iron. He was off his feet and being hurled through the air.

He crashed into a wall and lost consciousness. As he momentarily revived, shaking his head and driving the *chi* deep within himself to penetrate his entire being, he saw the Major's grinning face, and the hands that reached up to rip his eyes out.

Moon screamed. The Major was distracted. Mace gripped both hands together and smashed upward as hard as he could against the Major's larynx and connected. The Major reeled back, staggering.

Moon Chu Lingdoo, who had come out of the store room where she had been hiding, picked up the table leg and bashed at the Major's head. Hsung Fong was up, floundering past her, his face bloody from the blow. Mace blinked and saw him and tried to rise. He saw Moon following the Major into the store room through the open door. There was a crash. Moon disappeared. Mace could barely raise his head. Then he lost control and fell to the floor.

In the darkened confines of the store room against the formica topped counter Major Fong gripped Moon Chu Lingdoo's hair in his right hand and pulled her head back painfully. Her teeth had bitten a great chunk out of his cheek, and her nails had torn a flap from his forehead. He was bleeding profusely. His left hand, cupped in a Tiger Claw position, slashed at her right breast, tearing her dress and flesh away. He jerked at her hair. She screamed.

He thrust her against the formica top and bent her body over backwards, grabbing her throat from behind with his left hand and smashing his right, flat out, at her chest, forcing anguished screams out of her bleeding mouth. Moon fainted. Major Fong kicked her head as it slid down to the floor with his right foot, slamming her against the wall. Her skull caved in like a ripe melon. Mace was still alive, the Major thought, but he could be dealt with later. He had one job to do now, and he must do it alone, with Captain Galey dead. He reached over and flipped on the light switch so he could see what he was doing.

Mace heard Moon scream and shook himself to clear the clouds in his vision. He could not. Then, at the same instant, there was an ear-shattering, earth-shaking explosion that disintegrated the store room wall. It seemed as if the whole side of the building was going to go up with the store room.

The papers and shelves around Mace swirled into confusion, with broken sections of sheetrock and timber hurtling through the air. Crumpled lumber and huge coils of armored cable slammed every which way. Plaster exploded, lifting dust into the chaos around him. A blue flash blared and faded. Smoke rolled over him.

Mace had been hurled into the main office through the door by the force of the blast, but he had recovered enough to tuck in his head and tumble over backward two and a half times, coming to his feet in a crouch.

"Moon!" he shouted. Smoke rolled away. Fire licked at the area where a huge hole now appeared in the wall. The transmitter, for that was exactly what Mace had guessed was hidden in the store room, was no more.

Moon must have somehow destroyed it.

And herself. And Major Fong . . .

Mace could hear feet clattering on the floor behind him. He wheeled, rady.

It was Juarez and Plato.

"Hurry up," said Juarez. "Let's get out of here."

"But what—what—happened?" Mace wondered.

"The girl used the plastique. I *thought* she was smart."

"Your plastique?"

"I let her see it, I let her steal it," Juarez said

grimly. "Come on, Vic. Let's get out of here."

"*You—let—her—kill—herself—*"

Juarez grabbed Mace's arm. "Let's go, buddy."

Plato waved his arm toward the elevator.

"Damn you—" Mace began.

"She was finished here anyway," snapped Juarez. "Best to let her make amends for her stupidity."

"But—"

"We've got Dekker, and Bolton, and Galey. Now you don't want Houston Police to get Victor Mace, do you?"

Mace's head cleared.

"Let's go!"

They ran out through the doorway, entered the elevator, climbed up through the trap doors, made the roof, jumped down onto the lower section, went down through the maintenance elevator, climbed up from the basement and hopped into Lafitte's car.

"Where the hell is that spik and Lafitte?" growled Detective Keene, pacing back and forth in front of the elevator doors in the garage.

Gino shrugged. "Well, if they don't come down this way, Bateman will grab them in the building's lobby!"

Francois Lafitte's four-year-old Buick slammed around the corner of Travis and Clay on two wheels, ran a stop sign, and turned left on Crawford. Keeping his eyes out for black and whites, he sped up through town to Franklin and turned right, going under the Eastex Freeway and finally onto Navigation Boulevard, traveling east.

Still no pickup. He made the three miles to the end of Navigation Boulevard, and cut over through

Hidalgo Park to Harbor Drive, approaching the Turning Basin where Buffalo Bayou became Houston Ship Channel. At this point the wharves stuck out into the widened portion of the ancient bayou, and Houston Ship Channel began its fifty-two mile meandering route to the sea.

Sails of pleasure craft bobbed in the widened portion of the Bayou at the pleasure marina.

"Who are these birds I'm going with?" Mace asked Juarez.

"Two contract pros we've used in Caribbean deep-cover ops. They're good people, Vic. They'll put you ashore wherever you want to go in."

Lafitte kicked at the brakes, burned rubber off the tires and slewed to a dramatic stop.

They jumped out of the car and ran across the way toward the marina.

Mace could smell the good smell of sea water, of brine, of diesel oil, of fish, of seagulls. He sank down on the bunk of the forty-one foot motorized schooner *Lady Luck* and closed his eyes.

The deck rocked. Then Mace came awake. It was hours later. Benny Juarez stood in the companioway, looking down at him with beaming satisfaction. The C.I.A. chief of station raised his right hand, made an O with his thumb and forefinger, and winked.

"Galey's through for good—D.O.A. Bolton's in the slammer. He's got some explaining to do. Dekker's in the hospital. Shatford was found on the blown-out roof, wandering about. They recovered Major Fong's torso in the shambles down on the street beside the building where half the twenty-first floor ended up. Word has gone out quietly through Petroleum Institute channels to remove and destroy the detonators in every oil well lighter sent out by P.I. The oil crisis is over, amigo."

Mace's expression clouded. "And Moon?"

Juarez simply shook his head. Mace closed his eyes and said dreamily: "They are deep thinkers, busy, and devoted to their work. Usually they want to do more than they are able, and if they undertake a task beyond their abilities, they are disappointed when they discover they are unable to fulfill their objectives."

"What are you talking about, amigo?" Juarez wondered.

"It's Chinese lore," Mace responded, "the mythos of the birth date. Chinese believe in their horoscopes. I am reciting the traits and fates of those born in the Year of the Cock, which is, incidentally, this year."

"Major Fong? Captain Galey?" Juarez asked with astonishment.

"And perhaps Moon herself."

Mace leaned back and closed his eyes again, reciting slowly:

"They think they are right and know what they are doing. People of the Cock do not trust others, but prefer to do what they like alone. They are ambitious, deep thinking, but not far-seeing, and somewhat thoughtless. Although the People of the Cock present an image of high adventure to the world, they have little gift for it, and are instead filled with nonsensical plans that never mature."

"Amen," said Juarez. "And thank God for that!"

MURDER MASTER #3:
HOOKER SMASH OPERATION
by Joseph Rosenberger

Disguised as a Mack Man, Lou King had to jive in
Harlem to crack the Boss Pimp, who tied into the racket
that was blackmailing U.N diplomats. The third entry
in what has been called the best adventure series going
today!

12243—$1.25
